The Drifter

AMISH COUNTRY BRIDES

Jennifer Spredemann

© 2020

Published in Indiana by *Blessed Publishing*.

www.jenniferspredemann.com

All Scripture quotations are taken from the *King James Version* of the *Holy Bible*.

Cover design by *iCreate Designs* ©

ISBN: 978-1-940492-54-4
10 9 8 7 6 5 4 3 2 1

Get a FREE short story as my thank you gift to you when you sign up for my newsletter here:
www.jenniferspredemann.com

BOOKS by JENNIFER SPREDEMANN

*Learning to Love – Saul's Story
(Sequel to Chloe's Revelation)*

AMISH BY ACCIDENT TRILOGY
*Amish by Accident
Englisch on Purpose (Prequel to Amish by Accident)
Christmas in Paradise (Sequel to Amish by Accident) (co-authored with Brandi Gabriel)*

AMISH SECRETS SERIES
*An Unforgivable Secret - Amish Secrets 1
A Secret Encounter - Amish Secrets 2
A Secret of the Heart - Amish Secrets 3
An Undeniable Secret - Amish Secrets 4
A Secret Sacrifice - Amish Secrets 5 (co-authored with Brandi Gabriel)
A Secret of the Soul - Amish Secrets 6
A Secret Christmas – Amish Secrets 2.5 (co-authored with Brandi Gabriel)*

AMISH BIBLE ROMANCES
*An Amish Reward (Isaac)
An Amish Deception (Jacob)
An Amish Honor (Joseph)
An Amish Blessing (Ruth)
An Amish Betrayal (David)*

AMISH COUNTRY BRIDES
The Trespasser (Amish Country Brides)
The Heartbreaker (Amish Country Brides)
The Charmer (Amish Country Brides)
The Drifter (Amish Country Brides)

NOVELETTES
Cindy's Story – An Amish Fairly Tale Novelette 1
Rosabelle's Story – An Amish Fairly Tale Novelette 2

OTHER
Love Impossible
Unlikely Santa

COMING 2020 (Lord Willing)
The Unexpected Christmas Gift (Amish Christmas Miracles Collection)
Sequel to *Unlikely Santa* (title to be determined)

BOOKS by J.E.B. SPREDEMANN
AMISH GIRLS SERIES
Joanna's Struggle
Danika's Journey
Chloe's Revelation
Susanna's Surprise
Annie's Decision
Abigail's Triumph
Brooke's Quest
Leah's Legacy
A Christmas of Mercy – Amish Girls Holiday

Unofficial Glossary
of Pennsylvania Dutch Words

Ach – Oh

Bann – Shunning

Boppli/Bopplin – Baby/Babies

Bruder/Brieder – Brother/Brothers

Daed/Dat – Dad

Dawdi – Grandfather

Denki – Thanks

Der Herr – The Lord

Dummkopp – Dummy

Englischer – A non-Amish person

Fraa – Wife

G'may – Members of an Amish fellowship

Gott – God

Gut – Good

Jah – Yes

Kapp – Amish head covering

Kinner – Children

Kumm – Come

Maed/Maedel – Girls/Girl

Mamm – Mom

Ordnung – Rules of the Amish community

Rumspringa – Running around period for Amish youth
Schweschder(n) – Sister(s)
Wunderbaar – Wonderful

Author's Note

The Amish/Mennonite people and their communities differ one from another. There are, in fact, no two Amish communities exactly alike. It is this premise on which this book is written. I have taken cautious steps to assure the authenticity of Amish practices and customs. Old Order Amish and New Order Amish may be portrayed in this work of fiction and may differ from some communities. Although the book may be set in a certain locality, the practices featured in the book may not necessarily reflect that particular district's beliefs or culture. This book is purely fictional and built around a fictional community, even though you may see similarities to real-life people, practices, and occurrences.

We, as *Englischers*, can learn a lot from the Plain People and their simple way of life. Their hard work, close-knit family life, and concern for others are to be applauded. As the Lord wills, may this special culture continue to be respected and remain so for many centuries to come, and may the light of God's salvation reach their hearts.

PROLOGUE

Josiah Beachy whipped his cell phone out of his pocket and tapped to answer the incoming call. "Josiah."

"Hey, it's Jaden."

"Hiya, *bruder*. To what do I owe the pleasure?" he asked casually, but he knew a call from his Amish brother always carried serious implications.

"A letter came for you."

He shot out of his leather executive chair and strolled to glance out the window of his office from the twelfth story. "From whom?"

"It says B.M."

"B.M.? Any return address?" He frowned.

"No. But it looks like a hand-written letter. It's postmarked Indiana."

Indiana. If it was from Indiana, then...

"Hello? Josiah? Are you there?"

"Yeah. Yeah, I'm here. Listen, I'm not too far away. Will you hold onto it for me and I'll stop by and pick it up?"

"Sure. When?"

"Tomorrow." No, he didn't want to wait that long. Because if it was from who he thought... "Make that today."

"Today? Where are you?"

"New Jersey. Let's meet in our usual place." He scratched his head. "Around seven. Will that work?"

"*Jah*."

"Okay, see you then." He tapped his phone to hang up.

He squeezed his eyes shut. There was only one person in Indiana that he knew with those initials. His daughter. But it couldn't be her, could it? He feared this day might come...eventually.

The day of reckoning.

Josiah pulled his sportscar up to the small café, a place he and his brother had met at over the years in order to protect his secret. A secret he knew would ultimately come to light. A secret that would likely rip some people's worlds apart. Including his own.

His heart pounded as he walked toward the

entrance. He knew his brother parked his buggy in a lot a couple of blocks away, so as not to be seen. He spotted Jaden sitting on one of the comfy sofas inside the café.

He felt a smile forming at the sides of his mouth the moment he opened the door. No matter how much he loved his *Englisch* lifestyle, seeing his younger brother always rekindled a longing for home. Bittersweet memories indeed.

His brother stood and Josiah wrapped him in a bear hug.

"How's the family?"

Jaden shrugged. "*Mamm* and *Dat* are getting older every day. You should come home."

Come home.

It was what his brother told him each time. In fact, if you were Amish and you knew someone who'd left the fold, it was your duty to try to persuade the wayward person back into the Amish community. They believed your soul was in danger of hell fire, if you had been raised Plain but had chosen the ways of the world. Honestly, Josiah didn't know how he felt about all that. Surely, remaining Amish all one's life was not a requirement for salvation. Was it?

He shook off his thoughts and refocused on his brother. "Anything new?"

"Nah. Same ol'."

"You got a girlfriend or anything?"

Jaden shook his head.

"Working?"

"*Jah.*" Jaden blew out a long breath. "I'm...I'm thinking of leaving."

"The Amish?"

Jaden shrugged.

"Why? I mean, you've stuck with it this long. Might as well stay."

"It's boring. I mean, look at you. All fancy." He stared out the window, his eyes lighting up. "I bet that car can go pretty fast."

Josiah chuckled. "You have no idea. Wanna go for a spin?"

"Now?"

"Sure."

"I wish." Jaden shook his head. "I gotta get back. *Dat's* probably already wondering what's taking me so long. I'm supposed to be on an errand."

"And so you are." He cupped his brother's shoulder. "Just so you know, once you cross over and taste the *Englisch* life, it's nearly impossible to go back. So, unless you *really* want it, you might want to think twice. Your life will never be the same."

"In a good or bad way?"

"Both."

Jaden reached into his back pocket. "I guess I should give you your letter."

Josiah took the envelope, tapping it on his palm. "Thanks."

His brother shifted from one foot to the other. "What are you going to do?"

"About this?" He held up the envelope, twisting it between his fingers like a baton.

Jaden nodded.

"I don't know."

"It's from Bailey, you know. She's a sweet girl. It's a shame you never..." Jaden shook his head. "Well, whatever. It's your life. I'm not going to tell you how to live it."

Josiah swallowed the lump attempting to form in his throat. "I appreciate that."

"You gonna open that thing or what?"

"Maybe. But not here. Not now." Who knew what it might contain?

"Okay. Well, I guess I better scoot."

"It was good seeing you again, Jaden."

"*Jah*, you too." He lifted a hand as he walked out the door.

ONE

One month prior...

Bailey breathed in the fresh scent of the cool night air as she sat next to Timothy Stoltzfus in his buggy. She loved the smell of nature after a good storm. The clip-clop of other couples' horses leaving from the singing echoed in her ears as they all made their way out onto the main road.

She shook her head, still baffled that she was actually courting Timothy Stoltzfus—or, more accurately, he was courting her. This was their tenth buggy ride together, not that she was counting.

Oh, but she'd hated him the first several years of attending school together. He'd teased all the girls and made fun of them. He'd been sort-of mean. But then Bailey started taking *Dat's* advice. She befriended him by doing kind things for him, like helping him with his schoolwork when she'd finished hers early. They eventually became best friends. Well, the best an Amish boy and girl could get without raising too many eyebrows.

After they finished school they'd only seen each other during church events, so their friendship had fallen to the wayside as their individual lives became busy. But as soon as they began attending singings, Timothy had been the first boy to ask her to ride home with him. And he'd been the only boy she'd wanted to ride home with. Not only was he the same as he'd been when they left school, but he was even more handsome now that he was entering manhood. Their friendship resumed easily, but quickly turned into more when he'd kissed her on their fourth buggy ride, not that she was counting.

Now, she regularly had crazy ideas in her head about their future together. Because she was quite certain *Gott* intended her and Timothy to be together forever.

"Do you think your folks are still up?" His eyes sparkled under his black felt hat, as they did quite often when he looked her way.

"I doubt it. *Mamm, Aenti* Jenny, and I have a lot of baking to do tomorrow, so I suspect they turned in early."

Timothy guided the horse and rig into her driveway. They moved past their small store, which had grown larger since her *Onkel* Paul had gotten married and Aunt Jenny had started her bakery section. Which reminded her... "Do you want to try some of the new dessert my aunt Jenny made today?"

"I don't know. I thought we'd just go for a walk tonight." His voice lacked its usual enthusiasm.

Goosebumps prickled on her skin as she said the words. "Is...something wrong?"

"Not now. We'll talk about it on our walk, okay?"

So something *was* wrong. Bailey's mind spun in a million directions. What on earth could Timothy be mulling over? She tried to think of what it could be. Was everything okay at home? Was somebody sick? Was he sick? She eyed him from under her black bonnet. *Nee*, he didn't appear to be ill. Just serious. Overly serious.

She released a breath when he hopped down and tethered the horse to their hitching post near the barn. He often used this one when everyone was asleep, in case the horse whinnied and woke someone in the house. The hitching post near the house was more convenient, especially when the weather was foul. But the sky had been clear since the storms passed yesterday evening, leaving behind the fresh clean scent of nature mixed with wet asphalt.

"You want to walk along the road or in the fields?" he asked.

"It doesn't matter to me."

He reached for her hand. "Let's walk along the driveway, then we'll cut into the field from the road."

It was likely their friends were out driving on the road. This way, they'd only be on the road for a short stretch of time before they turned into their front field and they could avoid any buggies passing by.

"I was hoping to talk to you about something," Timothy began. "I don't know how this is all going to work out." He sighed.

"What do you mean?"

"Us."

"I don't understand." She glanced up at him.

"I discovered something recently."

"That was cryptic."

"Just hear me out, okay?" They turned into the field.

She nodded.

"I discovered that I'm in love with you, Bailey."

Her face warmed at his declaration. This was *good* news, right? So why did she feel nervous? Why did Timothy *seem* nervous?

"I love you. And I'm excited about it. I *was* excited

about it." He shook his head. "Anyway, I talked to my *dat*, and he and my *mamm* talked."

He stopped walking between the corn fields and turned to face her, taking her hands in his. "I don't know how to tell you this even. Bailey, my folks don't want me to court you anymore. They asked me to break up with you."

That hadn't been what she was expecting to hear. Her heart plunged as his words registered, and at the same time, tears pricked her eyes. "Do you always do what your folks ask?" She couldn't help her shaky voice.

"*Jah*. Don't you?"

She shrugged. "*Jah*, I guess so. Pretty much."

"I'm sorry." He reached over and brushed away one of her tears.

"Why? Why do they want us to break up?"

"Because you come from the *Englisch*."

"What?"

"They think you'll go into the *Englisch* world, because that's the way you were born."

"But I won't. I'm Amish now."

"I have a plan. I think we could just maybe break up for a while to make my folks happy. And then I can work and save up money. I don't have much right now. But once I turn twenty-one, I'll be able to keep everything I make and start saving *gut* money for a house for us. And by that time, we both will have joined the church, and hopefully my folks will see that you're set on staying."

"But I'm set on staying *now*. There's nothing out in the world for me. Everything, my family, is all here. I don't even know any *Englischers*. Why would I want to leave? Where would I even go?"

He shrugged. "I don't know."

"But twenty-one? That's a long time."

"Maybe more. I know. But three or four years isn't that long. And it will go by fast."

"Your folks will want you to court other *maed*." More tears dripped onto her *kapp* string and cascaded down her cheeks.

He crushed her close and kissed the top of her head. "I won't if I can help it. My heart only belongs to you, Bailey. It has since the first day you helped me with my schoolwork." He lifted her chin and met her lips with his.

Would this be the last night they kissed? If they broke up...

Ach, nee! She didn't want to think about it. She liked what they had. She wanted to stay right here— in Timothy's arms—forever. How could she wait *four* years? How could she stand by and watch Timothy court other *maed*?

12

He pulled back and stared into her eyes. "Say something, Bailey."

"What can I say? There's nothing I *can* say. You can't defy your folks. But what if they *never* change their minds? What if they *still* want to keep us apart after waiting all those years? What if I'm *never* good enough for them? For you?"

"You're *more* than good enough for me. Don't you ever think that you're not. You're the best thing that's happened to me, Bailey Miller. And I think our friends will agree with me on that. As for my folks, I'll be old enough then, and financially stable enough to make my own choices. If they're still against us, then I will choose you. And I'd choose you now, if I was able to strike out on my own. But I'm just not." His thumb caressed her jawline. "If you're working and saving money too, we'll get there faster. We can do this, Bailey. I know we can. It's just a bump in the road."

She nodded, feeling slightly reassured. "Just a bump. A very long bumpy bump."

He chuckled. "That's what I love about you. Well, *one* of the things. You make me smile."

"Will you still come see me at the store?"

"I don't know how I'd be able to stay away. I want to, but we'll have to be careful. If my folks suspect we're still seeing each other, it could go bad. And there are those who can't seem to keep their mouths closed, so we can't be seen together or they'll find out for sure."

"Should we still go to the young folks' gatherings then?"

"I don't think my folks would let me stay home. Would yours?"

She shook her head. "Probably not."

"Bailey." He frowned. "You won't ride home with anyone else, will you?" His voice was unsure, maybe even a little worried.

"You know I only love you. Why would I *want* to ride home with anyone else?"

He stared up at the sky and sighed. "*Ach*, I just wish I could go to sleep and wake up four years from now."

"Me too."

"But we can't, can we?" He took her hand in his again and they continued walking.

She shook her head.

"Do you ever wish your mom had stayed *Englisch*? Do you remember anything from back then?"

"Yeah, I remember some. And no, not really. There wasn't really much to miss. I was pretty young, so I think I adjusted well to becoming Amish. My grandparents died when I was young and we really didn't have any other close family. And then when we came here, I was just so happy that Silas was going to be my daddy—that I would finally have one." She laughed at herself. "And I got two more sets of new grandparents."

"Two?"

She stared at the corn stalks as they passed each one. "Yeah, *Dawdi* and *Mammi* Miller, Silas's folks. And my real father's mom and dad. The Beachys. They live in Pennsylvania."

"Do you ever wonder about your real dad? I mean, you said he was Amish, right? But he died?"

"That's the way the story goes. He and my dad, Silas, were good friends. He drowned when he was a teenager—before I was even born. I don't think he ever knew about me." She frowned.

"That's sad. Do you ever wish you could have known him?"

"I do. But I love Silas. He's been a good father to me. My life wouldn't be the same without him in it."

"*Jah*, he's a good guy."

"Which makes me wonder why your folks are worried about me. It's not like my mom wants to be *Englisch* anymore, my real dad was Amish, and Silas is Amish."

"I know. It's frustrating." He sighed heavily as they

came back around to the driveway. "I should probably go, but I don't want this night to end."

"I think it's probably morning now, ain't so?" They walked to his buggy.

"*Jah.*" He pulled her close to him and held her tight. His body shook slightly. Was he crying?

Bailey pulled back to see tears shimmering in his eyes. Eyes she'd never forget for as long as she lived.

"Timothy..." One of her own tears dripped onto her face, then rolled down her cheek. Just seeing him this way, in such a vulnerable state, made this all feel so final. Like they were saying goodbye for eternity.

"I don't...Bailey...my heart is already aching for missing you."

"I know. I feel that way too."

He kissed her long and hard. "Don't...don't ever forget me."

He reluctantly forced himself away and hurried to untie the reins. He practically jumped into the buggy.

Bailey watched as he commanded the horse, the clip clop of the horses hooves moving faster than they ever had out of her driveway. Carrying her beloved away from her.

Would it be forever?

Gott, please don't let it be.

TWO

This had to be the *l-o-n-g-e-s-t* Monday Bailey had ever experienced in her entire seventeen-year lifespan. Customer flow at the store had been decent, but each time the door jingled, Bailey's head snapped up in hopes that it would be Timothy. But it wasn't. Not that she expected him to come after their gut-wrenching night together. Their final night as a courting couple.

She'd been up for hours after he left, but eventually cried herself to sleep.

"Why don't you go to the house and lie down? You're tired. I can handle this." *Mamm's* hand on her shoulder startled her.

"Are you going to keep the *kinner* here with you, then?" Her gaze moved to her two youngest siblings.

"I can. Go ahead. Get some rest. Your dad is working in the shop with Uncle Paul, so the house should be nice and quiet." *Mamm* eyed her carefully. "You and Timothy must've had a late night, ain't so?"

Ach, she hadn't told her folks about their break-up. Her emotions had been too raw this morning, as they were now.

Bailey nodded. "*Jah*, I'm tired."

She removed her store apron and placed it on the wall hook, then leaned over and kissed her mother's cheek. "Thanks, *Mamm*."

After tossing and turning for thirty minutes with nary a wink, Bailey finally gave up trying. She snatched a snack from the kitchen. Bits and pieces of her and Timothy's conversation played over again in her mind, reminding her how much she missed her maternal grandparents, who had passed on.

She now thought of them, attempting to recall their faces, something once vivid in her mind's eye. *Ach*, she hadn't seen a photo of them in several years.

Bailey pushed open the door to *Mamm* and *Dat's* room, knowing *Mamm* wouldn't mind if she took a gander at their photograph. But where was it?

She glanced around the room and tried a couple of *Mamm's* drawers, finding nothing, then removed the double wedding ring quilt that covered *Mamm's* hope chest. The cedar chest had been a gift from *Dat*, but it had belonged to his first wife. He'd been a widower when they'd married.

Bailey always wondered about that. Did *Dat* ever think about his first *fraa* and the *boppli* they'd lost? He'd never once mentioned it to her, but *Mamm* had said something one time. It was one of those things no one talked about.

Kind of like the subject of her real father.

She knelt next to the large wooden chest and inhaled deeply the moment she opened the trunk's lid. *Ach*, how she loved the smell of cedar. The scent seemed to linger on each item she removed from the chest. *Mamm* and *Dat* had given her drawer sachets filled with cedar shavings for Christmas one year. She kept her favorite items in those drawers, so they'd soak in the aroma.

After removing several things, she lifted a manila envelope from the box. Written on the top was J.B. Were those initials? *Ach*, her real father's maybe? It had to be. She wasn't aware *Mamm* had anything about her father, so maybe she was mistaken. But who else could J.B. be referring to?

She sat cross-legged on the floor and eyed the closed envelope, now resting on her lap. Would *Mamm* mind if she opened it? If it was indeed referring to her father, whose initials were J.B., then she wanted to know what was inside. His obituary, perhaps?

Curiosity got the better of her and she unclasped the flap. She peered inside the gold paper den. *Photos?* She pulled out the black and white strip of photos. A much younger *Mamm* and a handsome young man, with a hair style cut just a little shorter than the Amish in their district required for the men, stared back at her. They looked so happy. In love.

Was that how she and Timothy looked when they were together? Correction, *used* to look.

Ach, they were even *kissing* in one of the pictures! Her cheeks felt like they were on fire. Did *Dat* know *Mamm* had these? Surely he wouldn't have allowed her to keep them. Would he?

She flipped the photos over for some clue of where and when they were taken. *East Coast. Kayla Johnson and Josiah Beachy,* dated the year before she was born.

It *was* her father! Now that she studied the photos, she could see that she resembled him. Probably more so than *Mamm*. She ran her fingers over the photos, tears pricking her eyes. What would it have been like to know him? He appeared to be content—they both did.

"Why did he have to die, *Gott*?" A tear slipped down her cheek as she held the strip of photographs to her chest. She'd never have a chance to know her father. She'd never get to hug him. She'd never get to

20

talk to him. She'd never get to...well...*anything*.

She sobbed for several moments, allowing her tears to fall, grieving her father for the first time. If only she could have met him. If only she could have heard his voice. If only she could tell him how much she missed him.

Was it a betrayal to *Dat*—Silas—to be having these thoughts?

She sat staring at the photos, mesmerized. It was her father!

A sound outside caused her to snap back to reality. What if someone came into the house? Into the room, while she was sitting here staring at photos of her *mamm* and real *dat*? Photos meant to be kept hidden. What would Silas say if he saw these? What if *Mamm* knew she knew about them?

She should put them back.

She really should, but she didn't want to. She wanted to cherish them. She wanted them—him—close so that she could look at him anytime she wished. She'd slide them back into the envelope, then take them to her room.

She hurried to return them, then noticed something else inside the manila envelope. *A letter? Ach.*

But there was no time to pull it out and read it right

now. Surely the family would be barging inside soon.

She hurriedly but carefully placed all the items back into *Mamm's* hope chest. Well, all the items minus the envelope with her father's initials on it. She then rushed to her bedroom to hide her precious possessions. It would have to wait until later—maybe when everyone else retired for the evening.

Then, and only then, would she discover what other secrets her *mamm* had been hiding.

THREE

It was an amazing thing, really. Since finding the envelope with her father's initials on it earlier, Bailey had scarcely thought about the situation with her and Timothy. Had *Der Herr* sent her a distraction so she wouldn't be saddened by their sudden break-up?

Either way, she couldn't wait until supper was finally over and she could gaze at her father's image again. And what about the folded paper she'd seen inside the envelope? What mysteries might that unravel? It had to be something of importance if her *mamm* had kept it all these years. Didn't it?

Shivers ran up her spine and prickled on her arms. It was almost like she'd unearthed a buried treasure and she was the only one privy to it. It was kind of like finding pieces to a puzzle and snapping them into place. Would it ever be complete? Would she be able to find all the pieces? What would her puzzle look like once it was complete? Would she be happy with it?

One thing was for sure and for certain. The photos of her father were like receiving a gift straight from Heaven.

"Bailey?"

"*Jah*?" Her attention snapped to her father. Or should she call him Silas? It was strange how she felt weird referring to him as *Dat* now that she'd seen a photo of her real father. It was like her father—Josiah—became real to her all of a sudden.

"You look like you're a million miles away. You haven't taken more than two bites of your supper." He frowned.

"I have a lot on my mind right now." She moved the food around on her plate with her fork.

"*Mamm* said you and Timothy had a late night?" His brow arched.

She glanced at the younger kinner, who had already been dismissed from the table. The two oldest, Judah and Shiloh, helped *Mamm* gather the dishes from the table.

"We did, *jah*."

"How was your nap?" *Mamm* stood near the table, their smallest *boppli* balancing on her hip.

Their boppli.

24

All of the *kinner*, except her, were fully part of this family. Did they love *her* any less because she hadn't come from the two of them? Funny she'd never considered that till now.

"Not *gut*. I couldn't fall asleep." She answered honestly.

"Maybe you should turn in early tonight, then," Silas suggested.

"*Jah*. I think I might do that." She frowned.

"Is everything okay, Bailey?" A worried look flickered across *Mamm's* face.

"I just...I should..." She might as well just say it. "Timothy and I broke up." Sadness filled her heart at the words.

"*Ach*, really? Why, Bailey?" Her mother gasped, but her words communicated the sadness that Bailey felt.

"His folks are afraid I'll go back to the *Englisch*." She hated that her voice quivered. Hadn't she'd cried enough already?

"What?" *Mamm's* voice raised.

"*Jah*, that's what he said. Since I was born an *Englischer* and all."

"That's ridiculous." Silas frowned. *Ach*, he really was a *gut*, caring father. Even though he wasn't her real *dat*. "You have no control over how you were born. *Gott* decides that."

"Besides, you were only half *Englisch*. Your father was Amish." Her *mamm* locked eyes with Silas, but she couldn't decipher their unspoken communication.

She suppressed the questions zipping through her mind, although she was dying for more information about her father. "I think I'll go to my room now, if that's okay."

"That's fine. But just remember that we're here if you need to talk," *Dat*—Silas—said.

Mamm whisked her plate away. "I'll cover this up in case you feel like eating more later, okay?"

"*Denki, Mamm.*" She rose from the table and did her best not to rush to her room.

Once inside her private haven, she closed the door, wishing it had a lock on it. She took her desk chair and moved it to the door. If anyone attempted to barge in without notice, she'd at least have a few extra seconds to conceal her treasures.

Her heart pounded as she grasped for the envelope under her mattress. Anticipation had been clawing at her since she'd spotted the paper inside. She brought out the photo strip once again, smiling down at her *dat*. She finally knew what her *dat* looked like! But it didn't take but a couple of seconds before she set it aside.

She reached for the paper inside and checked to see

if the envelope held anything else. Did it? *Nee*, it was empty. *Ach*, were these two items the only reference she had to her father? It would seem so.

She carefully unfolded the letter. *Ach*, it was to her mother. She didn't remember *Mamm* ever saying anything about corresponding with her father. She had just assumed that they'd met, fallen in love long enough to...well...and then he died. But maybe that wasn't how it happened?

So many questions.

Bailey began reading...

> Dear Kayla,
>   I'm sure this letter comes as a complete shock to you. Surprise, I'm alive!

Wait. *What*? She searched the letter for a date, but there wasn't one. "Keep reading," she mumbled to herself.

> I don't doubt that this revelation stirs up all kinds of feelings for you, and I won't blame you if you hate me.
>   I didn't know you'd gotten pregnant from our whirlwind romance. To tell the truth, I don't know what I would have done back then if I'd found out. I would have contacted you

sooner, but I lost your contact information. Nobody knew it, but I was bent on leaving the Amish at that time in my life and nothing was going to stop me. I went on to pursue higher education and have now graduated from college.

So, he's an *Englischer*?

I've only learned of our child and your present circumstances recently. My brother is the one who gave me this address. He is sworn to secrecy, so you don't need to worry about anyone finding out about my existence.

Since we have a child together and you're about to get married,

About to get married? "You mean, *Mamm* knew you were alive *before* she married Silas?" Bailey whispered. "You and *Mamm* could have gotten married then. We could have been a family."

I figured I was obligated to at least give you a choice. I'm guessing you're in love with my former best friend. You must be, because I don't know of any other reason you'd willingly join the Amish. Silas is a very good person and you will be happy with him. But, if for whatever reason, you have doubts or you don't really want to marry into the Amish church, I would be willing to help you raise our child. If you're content as you are, then I will walk away and you'll never hear from me again.

No! "Don't walk away, *Dat*." But *Mamm* was already in love with Silas...

You can be confident that Silas will be a good father to our child. I'm sorry, I don't even know if it's a boy or a girl.

If you want me in your life, respond to this letter as soon as you receive it. If you don't, then ignore it, get married, and live happily ever after. Whatever you do, do not let anyone read this (especially not Silas) until after you've been married a little while. Don't ask why. Just trust me on this one.

If you ever need to get ahold of me, my brother will have my information. My parents don't know I'm alive and I'd kind of like to keep it that way. No one in the Amish church, with the exception of my brother and now you, knows that I'm alive and well. I know it sounds wrong, but I have my reasons.

I wish you and Silas the best.

Josiah

Bailey sat open-mouthed, unable to comprehend all that she'd read. She read over the letter again. And then a third time.

So, did Silas know he was alive or not? Did *Mamm* ever write him back? He'd said that his brother had his information. Which brother? Did his folks still think he was dead? Or did they know and was everyone just pretending he was dead? Was it to keep *her* from finding out?

Ach, she felt like she had more questions now than ever.

But one thing she was pretty certain of. Her father was still alive!

FOUR

Her father was still alive! And out there. Somewhere.

Joy surged through Bailey's veins. There was a very *real* chance that she would get to meet her *dat*.

She didn't think she'd ever been more excited in her life. Except for when maybe Timothy Stoltzfus asked to court her. Or when he kissed her for the first time.

But this was different.

The question now was how would she get a hold of him? There had been no envelope for the letter, which meant no return address. Which brother knew about him? Was it Uncle Justin? Or Uncle Jaden? Or was it Uncle Joshua?

Nee, it couldn't be Uncle Joshua. He would have been too young back when *Mamm* married Silas. If

Bailey had been about five when her father sent the letter, that meant that Uncle Justin would have been about fourteen. Would he entrust his secret to a then fourteen-year-old? *Nee*, she wouldn't think so. So that left Uncle Jaden, who would have been seventeen, her own age.

Okay. She'd write a letter to Uncle Jaden, then. She could send a note saying that if he knew anything about her father, that he would pass along the sealed envelope that contained the letter she would write to her father.

She bit her fingernail. What if Jaden wasn't the right brother, though? What if he had no idea where her father was? What if the letter found its way into *Mammi* and *Dawdi* Beachy's hands and she gave her father's secret away? Worse yet, what if her father received her letter and didn't want anything to do with her?

Maybe she should just talk to *Mamm* about it. But no, then *Mamm* would know that she'd been rummaging through her hope chest. But if *Mamm* had the envelope the letter came in, then she would mail it to the right person at the right place. She'd figure something out.

Kayla reached down to loosen the corner of the fitted bedsheet that covered Bailey's top mattress. She always loved the feel of fresh sheets on the bed after they'd been laundered and hung out to dry in the sunshine. She did admit, however, that she occasionally missed having an electric dryer like the one she'd used when she'd been *Englisch*.

Ach, that seemed so long ago now!

She'd been happily married to Silas nearly eleven years. Eleven years. Where had the time gone? Bailey would soon be plunging into adulthood. Kayla had gone back and forth in her mind about talking to her daughter about her biological father, but could never find the words. But she *should* know.

Bailey hadn't asked many questions over the years. And Kayla wasn't surprised since Bailey believed her father was deceased. But Silas and Kayla knew the ugly truth about Josiah. And honestly, she resented having to live out a lie just to protect his identity and whereabouts. Wherever he was.

She pulled off the final corner, bundling the bedding into a large fluffy ball. But not before something caught her eye. The mattress had moved slightly when she yanked off the sheets and a narrow strip of vivid color revealed itself. She moved the mattress a little more, then pulled the item out from under Bailey's mattress.

Kayla gasped when she saw Josiah's initials and realized what she was holding. The secrets of the past. Her fingers trembled. She hadn't seen this in years. She opened the flap and pulled out the strip of photos she'd once cherished—it had been her only tangible memory of her and Josiah's relationship. Well, that and Bailey.

She quickly shoved the pictures back into the envelope. No sense in digging up old memories. Josiah had turned out to be very different than what she'd believed him to be during the week they'd spent together at the beach all those years ago. Occasionally, her heart still ached from the loss, but she never dwelled on it long enough to fester.

How long had Bailey had this in her room? And why hadn't she come to Kayla about it? And what had she been doing going through her mother's personal possessions? Without permission.

It looked like she wouldn't be needing to share the truth about Josiah after all. Because, if her daughter had read the letter inside the envelope, she already knew.

What did Bailey think? Was she upset? Hurt?

She squeezed her eyes closed and prayed for the best.

FIVE

Josiah held his cell phone to his ear and waited for the answering machine on the other line to beep. "Hey, this message is for Michael Eicher. It's Joe. Will you give me a call when you get the message, please? It's somewhat important. Thanks." He rattled off his cell phone number, then hung up.

Now the waiting game would begin. If Michael checked the phone shanty as often as his folks checked theirs, it could be a couple of days before he received the message.

Josiah had left work early, letting his secretary know he'd be out of town for an undetermined amount of time due to a family emergency. There was no sense in staying at work when he couldn't focus. She'd been taken aback by his comment, probably because he never mentioned his family. And unlike others in the offices around him, his desk wasn't cluttered with family photographs.

He owned exactly *one* photo album. One album that contained photos of his various adventures. It had once held appeal, but now? He'd come to realize that, without friends or loved ones at his side, those memories were meaningless. Worthless. Empty. They only served as a reminder of how lonely his life had become.

Which is why Bailey's letter meant the world to him. It stirred something in his heart. He wasn't sure exactly what he would do, but reconnecting with others from his past was now high on his priority list.

He now rummaged through his closet. Nothing but city clothes. That was something his brother had teased him about in the past. He could only imagine what onlookers thought when they spotted the two brothers at the café—one in dirty Amish clothing and the other usually in a fancy suit. No doubt they looked like odd ducks.

Fortunately he did own a couple pairs of jeans— albeit they were nice jeans. If he did visit Michael, he'd have to borrow some of his friend's clothing. Because if he intended to stay on an Amish farm, he didn't doubt he'd be expected to work. And even if he wasn't, he'd at least feel obligated to.

Bailey was in *big* trouble. The envelope with her father's letter and pictures was now missing. She racked her brain trying to remember if she'd moved it or hid it somewhere else. But no. She was *certain* she'd left it under her mattress. Which could only mean one thing.

Someone had discovered the envelope.

It had to have been *Mamm*. Bailey had seen the sheets drying out on the clothesline earlier in the day, but hadn't even stopped to think that they might be hers—or that they would disclose her secret to her mother. What would *Mamm* say? Or would she not say anything and wait until Bailey stepped forward and admitted the truth of her own accord?

"Bailey, when you're done with the dishes, please come into the living room," Silas said. "*Mamm* and I have something to discuss with you."

And there it was. Her mother and her father—Silas—wanted to talk to her.

She wasn't sure why, but her hands trembled. Was it from nervousness? Or excitement at finally getting answers to some of her questions? Perhaps it was a little of both.

Several moments later, she joined her parents in the living room.

After she took a seat, Silas began to speak. "I'm sure

you already know why we want to talk to you."

She could play dumb, but they would see right through it. "*Jah*. I think so."

Mamm held up the golden envelope. "Did you take this from my hope chest?"

"*Jah*. I didn't mean to find it. I was looking for pictures of Grandpa and Grandma Johnson because Timothy and I had been talking about them. And then I found that. Once I found it, I forgot all about the pictures of Grandma and Grandpa. I had no idea that you had anything from my father."

"So you looked inside?" *Mamm* asked.

"*Jah*."

Mamm and Silas glanced at each other. "And?"

"I was surprised. And a little confused." She frowned. "So, my father is *still* alive?"

"As far as we know," Silas said.

"I'm wondering why you never told me. I mean, if he's still alive, I could maybe meet him."

Mamm and Silas exchanged a look. "Do you *want* to meet him?"

She swallowed. "*Jah*. I mean, he *is* my father."

"*Dat* is your father," *Mamm* said.

"I know. But not really. He's my stepfather. I mean, I'm not adopted or anything, ain't not?"

"We didn't feel that was necessary. An official piece

of paper from the government has no bearing on the heart's decision. And we didn't want to have to ask your father to make that choice, to give you up," Silas said.

"So, did you think that he might come back to see me?"

Silas nodded to *Mamm*. "He actually did. One time. But you didn't know it was him."

"Wait. What? He came to see me? When?"

"It was after *Dat* and I were married. Josiah was going off somewhere—to another country or something is what I think he said—and he wanted to see you at least once."

"And he did?"

Mamm nodded. "For a very short time."

"Did he say anything? Did I talk to him at all?"

"*Jah*, he was amazed at how much you resembled him," Silas said. "He told you to be good for your *Mamm* and *Dat*. And I think you said that *Mamm* said you were a very good girl." Silas chuckled.

Bailey laughed. "I said that?"

They nodded.

"Is he still in another country?"

"We don't know. We haven't heard from him since. He said he was going to step out of the way, and he did."

"So, does everybody still think he's dead?"

"Mostly, as far as we know."

"Why does—did he want everyone to think he was dead?" Bailey frowned.

"Because he left the Amish. Instead of receiving letters from loved ones begging and pleading for his return and warning him that he was in danger of hell fire, he figured it would be easier to just drop off the face of the earth, so to speak. So that's what he did."

"But he wouldn't be in danger of hell just because he left the Amish, would he?"

"No. But some Amish do believe that if a person is a baptized member of the Amish church, for that person to leave would mean they chose the world over God, and that breaking the vow they made would damn them to hell."

Her eyes widened. "*Ach*, you said a bad word."

Silas's lips twitched. "*Nee*. It is not a bad word when used the right way, in the correct context."

"But that's wrong, ain't so? I mean, that they would...you know."

"Yes. Amish or not, the only thing that sends one to hell is unbelief. Rejecting Jesus. *He that believeth on him is not condemned: but he that believeth not is condemned already, because he hath not believed in the name of the only begotten son of God.*"

"Does my *dat* believe in Jesus?" Bailey looked at both of her parents.

Kayla shrugged. "I don't know, honey."

"I don't know either," Silas said.

"Well then, we have to tell him, right? Because we don't want him to...you know."

"No. We don't want him to. We don't want anyone to." Silas frowned.

Bailey bit her fingernail. *Ach*, she wanted to tell them about the letter she sent, but they'd probably be upset. *Nee*, she wouldn't tell them. At least, not yet. Really, there was no reason to right now. If her father responded, she could inform her folks at that time. Until then, she'd just wait and hope for the best.

SIX

Josiah nearly took a spill on the bathroom floor as he jumped out of the shower and lunged for his cell phone. He tapped to answer while simultaneously drying his face. "Josiah."

"Hey, it's Mike Eicher."

He noted the enthusiasm in his friend's voice.

"Wow, it's been forever. What are you up to these days? Still exploring the world?"

"Nah. Not anymore. Just working behind a desk, shuffling papers and pushing pencils all day."

Michael chuckled. "Sounds like a dream job."

"I literally just saw you roll your eyes in my mind's eye." He grabbed a clean towel and began drying his body.

"Wow, what are you? Psychic?"

"Did you really? You rolled your eyes?"

Michael laughed. "I did."

It was so good to chat with an old friend. "Hey, listen, I have a favor to ask."

"Sure. Shoot."

"You're in Indiana, right? Are you anywhere near Rexville?"

"You mean tiny little if-you-blink-you'll-miss-it Rexville? *Jah*, I actually go there quite often."

"But you're not in the same Amish district or anything, are you?"

"No."

"Okay, good. Uh, how would you feel like having a visitor for a little while?" He blew out a breath. "If it's an inconvenience, I can just stay at a motel in one of the nearby towns."

"You? You're coming out this way?"

He could hear Michael's smile over the phone. "That's the plan."

"That would be great. We'd love to have you."

"We?" Last he knew of his friend, he'd been a single playboy. But his brother Jaden *had* mentioned that Michael joined the Amish. Josiah should have figured there'd be a "we" involved.

"It's me, my *grossdawdi*, my *fraa*, and our *kinner*."

Josiah grimaced. "Oh. Well, I don't want to impose if you've already got a full house." Besides, he was used to living alone.

"Nonsense. The more the merrier. Everyone would love to have you."

"You're sure?" Not that he was surprised. Hospitality was the Amish way.

"Trust me."

"Thanks, man. I really appreciate it."

"When do you think you're coming out?"

"How soon can you accommodate me?"

"I'm sure my *fraa* would appreciate a day or so to ready a room, but you can drop in now as far as I'm concerned." He chuckled.

"If I leave in the morning, I'll probably take a couple of days getting there. Will that work?"

"Sounds perfect. We'll see you then."

Josiah clicked off the phone at the same time Maestro's meow echoed from the other side of the bathroom door. The feline had been a gift from his elderly neighbor next door, who owned several cats herself.

"Everyone should own a cat," Ms. Parker had said, when she showed up the week after he'd moved in to his condo, litter box and bag of cat food in hand.

How could he say no to that?

Which made him wonder. Did she do that for each new tenant? Or had she just taken pity on him because he showed up single?

Hopefully, Ms. Parker would be able to cat sit for him while he was gone. Because he couldn't see Maestro happily caged for hours on end. He was used to being home.

Dried and clothed now, he sat on the couch, flipping on the television. He surfed through several channels, but none of them caught his eye. Maestro jumped onto the sofa and rubbed his head on Josiah's arm.

"Come here, buddy." He pulled the cat onto his lap. "You gonna miss me while I'm gone? Ms. Parker has some lady friends next door that you can meet. They might be your sisters."

He mused on his comment. It seemed like eternity had come and gone since he'd seen anyone in his immediate family, save Jaden. How were his siblings doing? *Mamm* and *Daed*? How would they react if they discovered he was indeed alive and well?

He shook off the thought. He wasn't going to Pennsylvania. He was going to Indiana. Only Indiana. To see his only daughter for the second time in his life.

He slid his hand over Maestro's soft fur. "Wish me luck, Maestro. Tomorrow's the day I set off on this crazy journey. Who knows what the outcome will be? I certainly don't."

Josiah cringed the moment the red and blue flashing lights came on behind him. "What?" He glanced down at his speedometer. "No! Not again." He banged the steering wheel.

There wasn't enough room to pull over on the freeway, so he veered toward the first exit he saw. He slowly rolled his car to a stop and reached for his insurance and registration, then fished his license out of his leather billfold.

He lowered the window as the uniformed officer approached.

"Do you know why I pulled you over?" The officer eyed him suspiciously.

"I think so." But he wasn't going to give it away just in case he was wrong. He could possibly have a taillight out or something.

"I clocked you at eighty-eight. The sign you just passed read sixty-five." He pointed back behind them. "License, insurance, and registration, please."

Josiah winced as he handed the documents over. "Really? I thought it was seventy-five through here." Which technically would have still been speeding. His fine would be sky high.

"Looks like you need to take some of that lead out of them shoes." The officer chuckled.

"Or get a different car," he mumbled, watching the

officer walk back to his patrol vehicle. While he loved his sportscar, it had too much power for his own good. He didn't know how many times he'd been casually driving, then glanced down at the speedometer to discover he was doing close to a hundred. Thankfully *this* hadn't been one of those times.

Several minutes later, the officer returned and handed him back his documents. "Where you headed?"

"Indiana."

"The Hoosier state." The officer nodded. "This is your lucky day. I'm gonna let you off with a warning."

Really? "Thank you." He swallowed his gratitude.

"You got any kids?" the officer asked.

"Yeah. A daughter."

"Take some of the money you just saved and buy her an ice cream cone." He tilted his stiff hat slightly with his hand. "Drive safe."

Josiah glanced at his side mirror as the officer returned to his patrol vehicle.

He stared out the windshield, blinking. He just dodged a ticket. A big one. "Woo hoo!" He turned over the ignition, then maneuvered back onto the road from the shoulder.

After Michael merged onto the freeway, now driving the acceptable speed limit, the police car passed him.

"Wow."

And now he owed his daughter ice cream. Would she even *want* it?

If she was anything like her mother was back when he'd last heard from her, she'd likely take the cone and shove it down the front of his shirt. To say Kayla had been upset was an understatement. More like steaming mad, judging by the vehement words she'd composed in her short letter back to him.

What had it been? Twelve years now?

In all that time, had she been able to find it in her heart to forgive him? For her own sake, he hoped so.

As Josiah lounged against just a few of the five hundred pillows on his motel room bed, he reached for his daughter's letter. How many times had he read it since Jaden had handed it to him? His focus moved to the opening greeting.

Hello, Dad.

That was all he'd had to read before he'd lost it. It hit him squarely between the shoulder blades and had gone straight through, just like an arrow. He'd never been very emotional. But just seeing that one word—*Dad*—for the first time in reference to *him*. He. Was. A. Father.

And yeah, he'd known it for quite some time now. But to see the words in ink, written by his own flesh and blood. It messed him up.

He shoved away the blasted tears and continued reading the beautiful piece of his daughter's heart.

Is it okay if I call you "Dad"? Or would you rather I call you Josiah? Although, I think Josiah would feel weird to me.

He stopped and chuckled. She obviously overthought things. Did she get that from her mother?

As of right now, nobody knows that I found this letter in Mom's hope chest. It was with pictures of you and Mom.

He paused. The only pictures he remembered were the cute black and whites they'd taken in one of those three-minute photo booths in the boardwalk arcade. He smiled at the memory. Kayla had been gorgeous. Still was, last he saw her.

Even dressed as an Amish woman. And married to his former best friend.

That was still something he had a hard time getting over. Not that she'd married Silas, but the Amish part. Here, he had done everything he could to *leave* and become *Englisch*. Whereas she, an *Englischer* with all the freedom in the world, *chose* the constrictive Amish lifestyle. Of course, he knew she would have never chosen it if love hadn't been involved. He sighed. Silas was a lucky man.

He hoped that Bailey didn't have any notions about him getting back together with her mother. Because that is something that would never happen, apart from a tragedy. And Silas and Kayla really were good for each other.

I want to meet you. Is that possible? I don't even know where you are, but you wrote in your letter to Mom that your brother knows how to get a hold of you. I figure you must have been writing about Uncle Jaden, taking into account when it was written.

Anyway, I work in the store on Mom and Silas's property. I'm usually there by myself on Thursday mornings. It's usually pretty slow then. If you wanted to stop by one day, say between nine and eleven, that would be ideal.

If you don't want to meet me, I will understand. If you decide you don't want to, maybe you could just send a vague postcard or something? Write something like No Go, and I'll get the message.

But I hope you will. I'll be waiting.

Your daughter,

Bailey

"If I don't want to see you?" He chuckled. "Of course I want to see you, kid."

He'd had a half dozen scenarios in his head about how this could potentially turn out. Since she said her folks didn't know... He sighed.

Yeah, that couldn't be good. Both Silas and Kayla had been shocked when he'd shown up the first time when Bailey was...what? Five? Six? Which would make her right around seventeen now. About the age her mother probably was when he'd met her—when Bailey had been conceived.

Which made him wonder. Did his daughter have a boyfriend? And if she did, was she thinking about joining the Amish church and marriage and settling down at such a young age? For whatever reason, that didn't sit well with him. Not that he had any say-so in his daughter's affairs. But she should have a chance to experience life first, before making a lifelong commitment she couldn't get out of.

Hmm... Maybe he could help her with that—let her get a taste of something other than what she's always known. Not to show her anything immoral or anything like that, just that she has more than one choice. Because if she saw both sides, when she did finally decide which path to choose, she would do it with a clear conscience and have no regrets.

No regrets? Is that what you're telling yourself? He shook off his thoughts. No, he didn't have any regrets about leaving the Amish. He regretted the way he'd left—the cowardly way. And he regretted not taking Kayla's information with him. If he had...

No, he wasn't going to allow himself to go there. Not today. Not this time.

SEVEN

Bailey arranged the items on the baked goods shelf, then glanced up at the clock on the wall. Today was Wednesday, which meant tomorrow was Thursday—the day she'd told her father she'd be working alone in the store. Who knew if he had even received her letter, though. And if he *did* actually show up, would it be this week, next week, or some other date in the future?

She hadn't received a postcard saying he wouldn't come, but that didn't necessarily mean that he would.

The bell jingled over the door and she startled. *It's only Wednesday*, she reminded herself. She looked up to see Timothy.

"Hiya, Bailey."

She felt warm all of a sudden. "*Ach*. Hello, Timothy." She looked past him. "Did you...are you here alone?"

"*Jah*, of course. I wanted to see you. I've missed you." He stepped closer.

"I've missed you too." Probably not as much as she should have, though. She'd been too preoccupied with thoughts of her father and the possibility of a visit from him. She wished she could share everything with Timothy. But if her father wanted to conceal his identity, in order to keep his secret, it wouldn't be a *gut* idea to be telling people about him. *Ach*, it was certainly a sticky situation.

"What have you been up to?"

Mostly daydreaming about my father. She shrugged. "*Ach*, this and that. Working in the store, mostly. How about you?" She continued arranging the items on the shelf.

"Will you stop for a minute, please. I want..."

"Sure."

He looked beyond her. "Is anyone else here?"

"*Nee*, just us."

"*Gut*." He stepped near and wrapped her in his strong embrace. To her delight, his lips met hers.

But she hesitated and stepped back. "I thought we were...your folks...wouldn't they be upset if they knew you were here?"

"I don't know if I can stay away from you, Bailey. I can't stand not seeing you."

"What can we do?"

"We can maybe still see each other in secret. I feel like who I court should be my choice, not my folks'."

"But you'd be defying them, Timothy. Is that a good idea?"

"All I know is that it's not a *gut* idea for us to be apart."

"They say absence makes the heart grow fonder."

He chuckled. "If I didn't know any better, I'd think you were siding with my folks."

"I'm not. I just...sometimes it's hard to know what the right thing to do is, ain't not? I mean, if we get caught, they might think that I was leading you to disobey them."

"If we get caught, I will accept full responsibility."

"You're sure and certain they won't despise me?"

"No one could despise you, my beautiful Bailey." His thumb traced her jaw before his lips lowered to hers.

Ach, she hadn't realized just how much she missed her sweetheart until now. If only the two of them could marry and start their life together within the next year or two. It would be so *wunderbaar*! What would it take? How could they make this work? Obviously, they'd both need to be baptized into the church. But if they voiced their intentions, the deacon would go to their folks for approval. And if his parents were against them, against her...she just didn't see how they'd be able to pull this off.

"Uh, Bailey?"

They broke apart at the sound of the masculine voice. *Silas.*

Not just her face, but her entire being must be on fire. They'd never kissed in front of anyone. "Silas, uh, *Dat*?"

He frowned. Was it because she'd called him Silas and not *Dat* right away? Or was it because she and Timothy had been found in a lip lock? Or because she was supposed to be working? Either way, she was likely in deep trouble.

"Uh, Silas." Timothy took a step further away from her. "I apologize. It's my fault. I just missed Bailey and..."

Silas held up a hand. His eyes shot to Bailey. "You're supposed to be working. What if someone else had come in? It wouldn't look *gut*, you two like that."

Bailey swallowed. "*Jah*, I know."

He turned to Timothy. "Bailey mentioned that your folks weren't happy about you courting her."

"*Jah*."

"I can't condone you two going against your folks'

58

wishes. Kayla and I have nothing against you and Bailey dating, but this will not put either of you in their good graces. It would probably only strengthen their position against Bailey."

"But it's not fair," Bailey protested. "We love each other. Shouldn't we be able to decide whether we want to court each other?"

"I know what you're saying, Bailey. And that's why your *mamm* and I wouldn't interfere unless we thought you were in danger or making a very poor decision." Silas rubbed his beard. "But it's best if you respect Timothy's folks and obey their wishes. They are Timothy's authority that *Der Herr* has placed over him. Pray about it and let *Gott* work it out for you. Long suffering and patience are virtues we all must learn."

Timothy and Bailey frowned at each other.

Silas continued, "I know it's not easy, but following God's way is best. Trust me."

Timothy sighed. "He's right, Bailey. I shouldn't have come."

"*Der Herr's* timing is perfect," Silas said. He moved to the door to exit, then turned back. "The reason I came out is to tell you *Mamm* wanted you to bring back some noodles along with the leftover baked goods when you close up later."

"Okay."

Silas waved to them as he stepped out the door.

"*Ach*, I did not expect your *vatter* to show up."

Bailey almost blurted out that Silas wasn't her father, but caught herself. "Me neither."

"I thought for sure he'd say something about me kissing you. I'm glad he didn't."

"I'm pretty sure he and my *mamm* kiss a lot. I've caught them a few times." She vaguely remembered the first time she discovered them in the kitchen, back when she and *Mamm* turned in to seek shelter from a scary storm. It was the first time they'd been in an Amish community. And Silas was the first Amish person she'd ever met. But back then, she hadn't known there was a difference between Amish and *Englisch*.

"I guess this has to be goodbye, then. At least, for a while?"

Bailey shook her head, her tears threatened. "I don't want to say goodbye. Again."

"It's just temporary. I promise you we will get back together. You can hold me to that."

"I will."

He swiped one of her tears away as he pressed his lips to her forehead. And then he turned and walked out the door.

EIGHT

Josiah drove slowly down the country road, his tires spewing dust as he went. Maybe washing his sportscar before the trip hadn't been such a wise idea. He slowed each time he passed a mailbox. Didn't anybody put their name and address on their mailboxes anymore? How on earth did the mailman know who lived where?

He just hoped he was on the right road. His GPS had lost its signal shortly after he turned off the main road and onto a dirt road. The area was beautiful with the canopy of trees covering the rural road. He wondered what kind of wildlife inhabited the woods. A couple of deer had crossed his path about a mile back. Where was civilization? He could be in Timbuktu for all he knew.

"Well, I'll be." He spotted an Amish woman walking up ahead. Finally, someone he could ask. But would she talk to a strange *Englisch* man? He didn't wish to frighten her. Perhaps he should employ his Pennsylvania Dutch.

He pulled up beside her and inched forward as she walked. "Excuse me, I'm lost. You wouldn't happen to know where Mike Eicher lives, would you?"

"Michael Eicher?" Her eyes livened, and he was drawn to them immediately.

"Yes, that's right." He nodded.

"I'm headed to Michael and Miriam's right now."

"You are? This must be my lucky day. Is it far?"

"Just another mile or so." She'd said it as if it were no big deal.

"A mile?" He stared straight ahead. "How about if I give you a lift and you can show me where they live?"

"Uh…" She hesitated.

"It's no problem, really. I'm staying with them for a little bit. Michael and I grew up in the same district together."

"You were Amish?"

"Yes."

She nodded. That seemed to put her mind at ease. "Alright."

He stopped the car, put it in park, then rushed around to open the door for her. "I'm Joe, by the way. Joe Beachy."

She shook his proffered hand. "I'm Elnora. Elnora Schwartz."

"Nice to meet you. So, do you live around here?"

She nodded and pointed in the direction she'd come from. "Just up the road a ways."

He shut her door, then ran around to the driver's side. "Have you known Mike long?"

"His wife and I are friends."

"And have you lived here your whole life?"

"*Jah*. Pretty much."

She turned to him and he marveled at her high cheek bones, which he hadn't noticed before. She was a *very* nice-looking woman, he acknowledged.

"You said you and Michael grew up together. That was in Pennsylvania, right?"

He shook off his thoughts. He was not here to examine beautiful Amish women. "Yes. We both left in *rumspringa*, I believe. I know Mike came out here to live with his grandfather. I think his parents lived here for a while too, but they ended up moving back to Pennsylvania, is what I heard."

"Something like that. He's been back here several years now."

"Yeah. I was a little surprised when my brother told me Mike had gone back and joined the Amish here in Indiana."

"So, you still have contact with your family in Pennsylvania, then?"

"Just my brother." He grimaced. This ship was beginning to sail in deep waters. But, for whatever reason, he felt comfortable talking with Elnora. Not that he would divulge his secrets to her.

"Are you in the *Bann*? I mean, I'm sorry if that was a nosy question." She shook her head.

"No, I'm not." It wasn't a lie. "I left before I was baptized."

"But you're not in contact with your parents? Are they still living?"

"They are. And no, I'm not in contact with them." He attempted to keep his answers as concise as possible. Nobody needed to know his family believed him to be dead.

"Your family must miss you. I couldn't imagine not having contact with my folks."

"Our situation is complicated."

"*Jah*, there seems to be a lot of those situations among the Amish."

If she only knew. His was certainly one of the worst.

"Are you visiting Michael long?"

"I'm not sure yet."

"Are you visiting for any specific reason, or are you on a holiday?"

This woman was certainly a curious one! But he liked it. It meant she was probably pretty smart. After all, asking questions was how one learned. "Honestly, yes, I'm here for a reason. But I haven't really figured everything out myself yet."

"That sounds...mysterious." She laughed.

"Are *you* visiting Michael's family for a particular reason?" He turned the question around on her with a smile.

"As a matter of fact, Miriam is watching my *kinner*."

"So, you have children?" He briefly eyed her figure. "I never would have guessed."

She laughed. "These dresses hide a lot."

"So, do those *kinner* come with a father and husband?"

"They did. Andy passed on two years ago."

"Oh. I'm sorry to hear that. Are you thinking of remarrying, then?" It was quite common for widows and widowers to remarry within the Amish communities he knew of.

"Not really. I mean, I might if the right person were to come along. But there are only so many options for a widowed woman, if you know what I mean. I don't want to marry anybody just because I need someone to help me raise my children."

"I'm sure that trying to fill the shoes of another is a difficult task."

She nodded. "Andy was a good husband and father, for the most part."

"I'm glad to hear that. How did he die?"

"It was a freak accident. He was working for one of our *Englisch* neighbors, driving one of those large pieces of machinery. He was on a hill and the thing flipped over. It landed on top of him and killed him instantly." She brushed away a tear.

"Oh, I'm so sorry." He reached over and squeezed her hand. "How terrible."

"*Jah*. I was sad for myself, but telling the *kinner* was the hardest part."

"I can imagine."

She loosened her hand from under his and pointed. "It's just up ahead on the left there." Had her cheeks been this rosy before?

He turned into the driveway of a simple but adequate white farmhouse. The breeze kicked up and Josiah spotted blue curtains fluttering just inside the screened windows. For a moment, he pondered the absurdity that some Amish districts didn't allow for screens on the windows. *How on earth did they keep the insects out?* At any rate, he was glad Michael's district apparently was not one of them.

As his vehicle rolled to a stop in front of the house, his eyes meandered to a large barn that towered several hundred yards away. Beyond it, horses grazed in the pasture. It all looked so serene—and foreign to the city life he'd lived for the past decade.

He stepped out of the vehicle, stared up at the bright blue expanse dotted with cottony clouds over his head, and inhaled deeply. Nothing like the smells of the farm—fresh cut grass, alfalfa hay, wildflowers of all kinds, and, of course, manure. He couldn't say that he'd missed that part.

"Josiah Beachy. I never thought I'd see the day." Michael practically careened into him, engulfing him in a bear hug. "It's been a long time."

"I still can't believe that *you're* Amish. You said you were never going back." He cuffed his arm with a loose fist.

"Like you, right?"

Josiah nodded.

"Well, God sometimes has a way of making us eat our words." He pulled a pretty Amish woman to his side. "Meet my wife, Miriam. I call her Miri. And our kids are around here somewhere."

"Nice to meet you." Josiah offered a hand, which she shook.

Michael continued, "And I see you've met Nora."

His eyes widened. "Oh, Elnora. Yes. She was kind enough to show me the way." He briefly locked eyes with her.

"My friends call me Nora," she said.

"Well, then. I hope you'll come to consider me a friend." His smile was easy around her for some reason. "Nora."

Josiah noticed that Nora exchanged a look with Michael's wife, Miri.

"Well, we'll let you two catch up." Miri linked her arm through Nora's, pulling her toward the house. Their heads tilted together as whispers and a giggle floated through the air before reaching Josiah's ears.

Michael chuckled. "It looks like they have a lot to talk about."

"Yeah, it appears that way." Josiah smiled.

A boy in his mid-to-early teens, Josiah guessed, approached. His shirt and pants were dirty, as if he'd been working since sunup. He looked to Michael, then at Josiah's sportscar, and lifted a brow.

"This is my oldest son, Mikey." Michael said. "Mikey, this is one of my old friends from school, Josiah."

Josiah smiled. The boy was the spitting image of his father. "Nice to meet you, Mikey."

His eyes lit up. "Can we go for a drive in that thing?"

Michael chuckled. "I think your *grossdawdi* would have something to say about that."

"Ah, you're right." He sighed. "I know, it's *verboten*."

"It's only *verboten* for you to own it and drive it yourself. I'll see if I can't convince *Grossdawdi*." Michael winked at his son. "And your *mudder*."

"For reals, *Dat*?" He threw his arms around Michael. "Thanks!"

"You go wash up now. I'm sure your *mamm* will be putting supper on the table soon."

Mikey nodded and practically sprinted to the house.

Josiah chuckled. "I remember when I had that kind of energy."

"I know, right?"

A horse and buggy drove into the lane and headed for the large barn. "Looks like *Dawdi* Sammy is back."

Michael moved to the back of Josiah's vehicle. "You have a bag in here? We better get you settled."

Josiah popped the trunk open with his key fob. "I can get it."

"Nah, let me." Michael smiled. "Miri would have a fit. She's been training me in hospitality for almost a decade."

Josiah looked back to the house, where Michael's son had just disappeared a moment ago. His brow

69

furrowed. "*Only* a decade? But I thought...I mean, your son...how old is he?"

"Almost fourteen." Michael grimaced. "You're not the only one who had a *boppli* out of wedlock."

"Ah." Josiah cupped his shoulder. "I guess that would make us the rebellious ones."

Michael shook his head. "We *used to be* the rebellious ones. I've changed my ways. I'm hoping you have too."

Josiah blew out a breath. "Let's just say I'm working on it. That's why I'm here."

Michael nodded. "Have you seen her yet?"

"No." He exhaled, then stared out into the field, hoping he wouldn't tear up in front of his friend. He swallowed down his emotion. "Tomorrow."

"It looks like we might have some praying to do then."

Praying? Yeah, Michael had surely changed.

The older man walked up to them, a shopping bag dangling from his hand.

"Meet my *grossdawdi*, Sammy." Michael smiled and lifted Josiah's luggage. "I'll take these bags inside."

Josiah watched Michael disappear into the house, leaving him to introduce himself to his grandfather. So much for hospitality. He chuckled to himself.

He reached his hand out. "I'm Josiah."

Sammy's eyes narrowed as he took in Josiah's clothing, his grip strong. "You haven't come to tempt Michael in *Englisch* ways, have you?"

Josiah's smile faded. He got the feeling Michael's *grossdawdi* was a force to be reckoned with. "No, sir."

Sammy eyed his sportscar. "Let's keep it that way. He has a family now."

"I completely understand. That's actually why I'm in the area. I have a daughter that lives not far from here. I've come to see her."

"We'll see about that." He led the way into the house and held the door open for Josiah to enter first.

This was going to be an interesting visit.

NINE

"Okay, tell me *everything*." Miriam sat across the table as she and Nora enjoyed a little quiet time. The younger children napped, while the older ones played outside on the swing set Michael and Sammy had constructed.

Nora didn't miss the excitement in Miriam's voice. She shrugged. "There's nothing to tell."

"Oh, no. There's *definitely* something to tell. I saw the way you and Josiah were smiling at each other as you got out of his fancy car."

"We were just talking."

Miriam tapped her fingers on the table. "About what?"

"I don't know. Everything, I guess."

"Like what?"

"How we both know you and Michael. Where he's from. Andy's passing."

"You talked to him about Andy?" Miriam gasped. "This is better than I thought."

"What do you mean?"

"You don't hardly talk about Andy, to anyone."

"Well, he asked if I was married."

Miriam's eyes practically jumped out of their sockets. "He asked if you were married?" Did her voice just screech?

"Shh...you're going to wake the *kinner*."

"*Ach*, I'm sorry," she whispered. "But seriously? He asked if you were married? He has to be interested."

Nora sighed. "No one is going to be interested in me."

"Why would you say that? What about Marlin King?"

"You are making my point."

"So, he's two decades older. I'm just saying that there are people interested."

"*Jah*, because they want a *fraa* to look after them and provide for their needs."

"Is that so bad?"

"When that's *all* they're looking for, *jah*."

"You're right. But Josiah doesn't strike me as that type. I mean, he's Michael's age and still single."

"Which means he's likely set in his ways. And he

has secrets." She stared at her friend.

"But a man of mystery is intriguing, ain't not?" Miriam winked. "I guess it's okay to tell you what I know. You'll likely find out anyhow."

"What?"

"Michael said the reason he's here is to visit his daughter."

"Wait. He has a daughter?"

"She's seventeen."

"Seventeen?" She counted on her fingers. "Which means he would have been...?"

"I don't know. Maybe nineteen or so when..." Miriam let her voice trail off.

"Oh wow. That's younger than Michael was when you, well, you know."

"*Jah.*"

"So, he never married, then?"

"Not that I know of. Doesn't sound like it. I really don't know the whole story."

"Has he been *Englisch* ever since then?"

"I'm not sure." Miriam shrugged. "I'll see if I can find out more from Michael tonight."

"*Ach*, so he *is* a man of mystery."

"Seems so."

The trip had gone pretty well so far, Josiah decided. Especially now, as he sat at the supper table with a small army of what he would consider friends— Michael and his family, along with Nora and her daughters. It had been too long since he'd enjoyed this kind of fellowship. He'd been too busy to realize how lonely and boring his life had actually become.

His mouth watered as he forked another bite of the pot pie. The flaky buttery crust practically melted in Josiah's mouth.

"*Gut*, ain't so? Makes your tongue wanna slap your brains out." Sammy grinned.

Josiah guffawed. "I guess that's one way to put it."

"I'm afraid I'm addicted to Kayla's pot pies."

Kayla? "I could see how one could get addicted to these things." He turned to face Sammy. "Who did you say makes them?"

"Kayla Miller. Lives not too far from here. Rexville area. Married to Silas Miller."

Have mercy, Lord.

Josiah suddenly felt Michael's gaze boring into him, and he turned his way. Their eyes connected and silent communication passed.

"Josiah knows Silas. We were all friends once." Michael chimed in.

Sammy's brow jumped. "Once?"

"It's a complicated story." Josiah hung his head.

"Ooh." Sammy rubbed his hands together like a child about to receive a birthday gift. "The best kind."

"Let's save *that* conversation for another day. I'm sure Josiah is tired and he'd probably like to relax." Michael smiled. Bless him for saving him from what would surely be an awkward conversation. "Am I right?"

"Actually, a bed sounds really good. I'm beat." He stretched his arms, the motion causing his short sleeve shirt to strain against his biceps. He looked over to find Nora glancing his way.

"We should get going soon too," Nora said, dipping her head. She and Miriam had shared several looks when he and Michael had been conversing, but she'd only graced *him* with a glance a time or two during supper. Why was he disappointed by that?

Maybe because he'd enjoyed their previous conversation in his car. Or because he wanted to get to know her better? But why? She was plainly Amish. And he was not.

After Sammy finished the final meal prayer, Michael stood from the table. "I'll hitch up the buggy to take you home."

Josiah shot up. "I can drive them."

Sammy chuckled. "They won't fit in that tiny contraption of yours."

"I wanna ride in the car!" Mikey said.

"I meant in the buggy." He glanced at Sammy, then Michael, then Nora. "If that's okay?"

Mikey's excitement deflated.

Nora and Miriam exchanged another look. "Uh, *jah*, that's fine. I guess," Nora said.

Well, it wasn't exactly jumping for joy, but at least she hadn't refused his offer.

"Thought you said you were tired." Sammy chuckled again.

"A slow buggy ride will be relaxing. Especially in these parts." His gaze connected with Nora's. "The perfect way to end the day."

A shy smile lifted before she looked away. "I'll gather the girls."

TEN

Nora's gazed flickered to Josiah as he held the reins in his hand. She couldn't help but notice the muscles that rippled in his forearms at the motion—and when he'd stretched after supper. Josiah Beachy was a very good-looking man. *Englisch* man, she reminded herself.

He seemed like a really nice, easy-going guy. One that, if he were Amish, would make good husband material. But, of course, she wasn't in the market for a husband—Amish or not.

"That was some delicious dinner."

"*Jah.* Kayla's pot pies are famous in these parts. And you should try Jenny's cinnamon rolls."

"Jenny?"

"She's Kayla's sister-in-law. She and her husband Paul, Silas's brother, live next door to Silas and Kayla. She runs the bakery in their shop."

"It sounds like I need to stop by there." He glanced her way and smiled.

"Miriam said you were needing some Amish clothes."

He nodded. "Although, I don't think Michael's pants are going to fit me." He chuckled. "I'll look like I'm waiting for a flood if I wear his broadfalls."

She laughed. "I imagine so. My...uh...Andy was about the same size as you are. You're welcome to try on his clothing if you'd like."

His gaze softened as he stared at her. "That's...very thoughtful of you, Nora."

"I really have no use for them. I don't even know why I still have them."

"Maybe you were keeping them for me." *Ach*, had he just winked at her?

"I suppose that could have been *Der Herr's* plan, since he knows the future." What was to be her future, she wondered.

He glanced behind them. "It looks like the girls have conked out."

"It's later than what they're used to." She gestured up ahead. "Pull into the next driveway. This is our place."

He did as instructed. He maneuvered the horse to a hitching post, just off to the side of the front of the house. "Nice place."

"*Denki*. Andy built it."

"Looks like he did a fine job. So he was a carpenter?"

"No, not really. He actually worked in an RV plant up north."

"You mean, like Middlebury?"

She nodded.

"That's quite a ways to drive."

"He and some other guys would hire a driver. They'd stay up there all week, then return home on Friday." She frowned.

"Oh, wow. So you didn't really see him much then."

Was that why she didn't feel like she missed him as much as she *should* have after he passed? Because she'd been used to him being gone? "Not as often as I would have liked to. He wanted to move up there, but I didn't. I like where we live. And we hardly ever get snowed in. They get a lot more snow up north."

He hopped down and tethered the horse. "I'll help carry the little ones in so you don't have to awaken them," he offered.

"*Denki*. You may as well come in and try on those trousers."

"That sounds *gut*." He lifted her youngest *dochder* out of the carriage.

"*Gut*?" Her brow hitched.

He chuckled. "I guess you all are rubbing off on me."

Since her oldest *dochder* had woken up, Nora guided her out of the carriage and took her hand, as they walked to the house.

She opened the door, allowing Josiah to walk inside her dark home first. "*Ach*, let me light the lantern."

"I appreciate that. I'd hate to trip with this little one in my arms."

A soft glow penetrated the room once she turned up the wick. "Their bedroom is just over here." She walked across the living area, then entered her daughters' room. "The small bed is hers."

She whispered in her oldest daughter's ear and she climbed into bed.

He lowered the small child onto her bed, then bent down and kissed her cheek. He pulled the top blanket over her tiny sleeping body.

"I hope that was okay," he whispered. "I couldn't seem to help myself."

She stood by the doorway and he joined her. She pulled the door, leaving it cracked open like always. "It's fine."

"I just..." He shook his head and blew out a breath. "I'm sorry."

"Are you..."

"I'm fine. That just hit me right here." He put his fist over his heart. "My daughter...she's all grown up. I never had the chance to tuck her into bed like that. To kiss her cheek." He swept his hand over his eyes.

"Miriam mentioned that you had a daughter."

"I'm sorry. I never thought it would affect me this way, you know?"

She nodded. "Would you...I could put on some water for coffee or tea."

"That would be nice. Thank you."

She gestured to the kitchen table as she filled the kettle with water. "You may take a seat, then I'll fetch those pants for you."

He did as instructed.

She hurried to her bedroom closet and pulled out two pairs of Andy's work trousers. She remembered lovingly sewing each one for her beloved. They'd lasted several years and were still in good condition.

She brought the trousers into the dining room and handed them to Josiah. "The bathroom is the second door on the right. I keep a lantern on the counter in there."

"Thank you." He held the pants up. "These look about right."

As he disappeared behind the bathroom door, she pulled out the brownies she'd made earlier in the day.

She'd planned on having them for dessert tonight with the *kinner*. Since they'd been invited to take supper at the Eichers' place, her plans had changed. She placed two on a plate and set it on the table where Josiah had been sitting. They would go perfectly with the coffee.

"How do I look?" Josiah walked into the kitchen wearing Andy's trousers. He turned in a complete circle.

She hadn't expected him to come out and show her. But now that he did... "They look *gut*." Her cheeks heated. *Jah*, she *really* should not be examining how this man's pants fit him.

"The suspenders fit perfectly. And with boots on, the legs should be fine too. I think your husband might have been just a little bit taller than me."

Right. The suspenders. "Great." But the Amish attire looked ridiculous against his short-sleeved shirt. "Do you, uh, need a couple of work shirts?"

"Oh, that might be good. If you think your husband and I were about the same size."

"They should work." She nodded and hurried back to the bedroom. She returned and handed him two shirts.

"Thanks." He lowered the suspenders and peeled off his shirt. She'd expected him to go back into the bathroom, not change right there in front of her!

"*Ach*!" She spun around quicker that a fox being chased by a coon dog. Wouldn't it be something if the deacon or ministers or bishop happened to be walking by and haphazardly peeked into her window? Or worse yet, Fannie Mae, the one no one dared tell their secrets to.

"I'm sorry." He chuckled. "I'm just so used to...well...I go to the beach often."

Apparently shirtless, judging by his tanned torso. Not that she'd been looking.

"I didn't even think."

That was quite all right, because she was thinking enough for the both of them. *Oh my*. She didn't dare share this episode with Miriam.

"I...uh...the coffee's ready." Like she needed something that would raise her temperature even more. Ice cubes. She'd drop ice cubes into hers.

"Ooh...and are those brownies?"

She nodded, placing the kettle onto the table beside instant coffee and tea bags.

"You can look at me now." He chuckled.

"Are you sure?" She tamped down a smile, handing him one of the mugs.

He laughed now. "I'm sorry. I didn't mean to make you feel uncomfortable. Will you...join me?"

"*Jah*."

"Thank you again for the use of your husband's clothes."

Ach, she'd forgotten! "Do you need a hat too?"

"I wouldn't want to—"

"It's okay. He had several." As a matter of fact, he'd just purchased a new one the week before his death. The thought grieved her only a little bit now compared to the first few months after his passing.

"I appreciate it. Really." He reached for a brownie. "This is delicious."

She shrugged. "I can't take credit. It's from a box."

"I won't tell if you won't." He winked.

She needed to change the subject. "When do you plan to see your *dochder*?"

"Tomorrow, if all goes well." He grimaced.

"So, you...have you seen her before?"

"Once. She was about five or maybe six then."

"Oh, wow."

"Yeah. I just hope it goes well."

"What made you decide to come visit her?"

"She sent me a letter. She wants to meet me."

"Well, that's a *gut* sign. Right?"

"The thing is, I don't know if her parents know if I'm coming or not."

"Oh."

"Yeah, I guess she stumbled upon an old letter that I'd written to her mother. It's kind of a long story. But to sum it up, her mother is married to my former best friend."

"Oh. I can see now why you said it was complicated." She frowned. "I'm trying to piece it all together in my mind. Okay, so you and your daughter's mom had a relationship and then she made off with your best friend?"

"No. It wasn't like that at all. He didn't come into the picture until later. They met when Bailey was five."

"Bailey?"

"*Ach*, I probably shouldn't have let her name slip."

"You don't mean Bailey Miller, do you? Silas and Kayla's daughter?"

He grimaced.

"Bailey is *your dochder*? *You're* her father?"

He nodded and blew out a breath. "I am."

"But I thought...I thought her biological father was dead. And *you* are very obviously alive."

"I am."

"And Bailey's parents, Silas and Kayla, they *know* this?"

"That I'm alive? Yeah."

She massaged her temples. This was confusing. "I don't understand."

87

"Let's just say I've done a lot of things in my past that I'm not proud of. It's my own fault that Bailey grew up thinking I was dead."

"How could you...why would you *want* your *dochder,* or anyone, to think that you're dead?"

"I was young and dumb and very immature."

"But if Silas and Kayla knew...I think I'm missing a few pieces to this puzzle."

"Remember I told you that I saw Bailey when she was little? Well, that was when Silas realized that I was actually alive. He and Kayla were already married. But I'd wanted to see her, my daughter, at least once." He sighed heavily. "Kayla and Silas were about to get married when I discovered that we had a daughter together."

"So you never knew?"

"Until then, no."

"Why didn't she tell you?"

"She didn't have a way to get ahold of me. She hadn't even known I was Amish when we met. I felt like I couldn't give her my contact information because then my folks would find out that I had an *Englisch* girl. And I was likely going to leave the Amish." He shook his head. "Like I said. I was young and dumb."

"So you basically abandoned Bailey and Kayla?"

"I left that decision to Kayla. When I found out we

had a kid together, I told her I would be willing to help her raise it. But they were nearly married. I can understand why she chose Silas. I wasn't there for her. He was, and she'd already fallen in love with him."

"How sad." Tears pricked her eyes.

"Yeah, so I basically disappeared again. But then, when this letter from Bailey came. I don't know. Maybe it's a second chance for me."

"That's quite a story."

"Now, I'm just trying to make up for all the stupid selfish things I've done in my life. I'm starting with my daughter."

"I can't imagine what you're feeling, Josiah."

"Thank you for listening. I don't even think Michael knows all that yet. If you could keep it between us until I figure things out..."

"Okay, *jah*." It would be difficult not telling Miriam. They were best friends. They told each other everything. And she'd try to pry it out of her. "If you want to talk or anything...after you go see Bailey..."

"I might take you up on that. Especially if you have more brownies." He winked, then stood from the table. "I should probably scoot."

"Let me get that hat for you." As he walked toward the door, she jogged to the bedroom and retrieved Andy's straw work hat.

89

"Thank you, Nora." His eyes locked on hers. "I've enjoyed this evening with you. Very much."

She let her gaze fall to the floor. "Me too."

He lifted his hand, then slid the back of his fingers over her cheek. Would it be wrong to close her eyes and lean into his touch? "Goodnight," his voice escaped as a husky whisper.

Her heartrate increased as she stepped outside and watched him walk through the darkness to the buggy. He waved with a smile as he set off down her driveway.

A breeze picked up, blowing her *kapp* strings. Like a kiss from *Gott*.

She wouldn't have imagined today if she'd dreamed a thousand dreams. She lifted her face, delighting in the cool air.

"What are your plans, *Gott*?" She whispered on the wind.

ELEVEN

"Well, I reckon you two are probably wantin' to chit chat." Sammy stood from the table and drained his coffee cup before putting it in the sink. "I'll be out on the porch swing with the Good Lord until you're ready to work."

"Thanks, *Dawdi*." Michael chuckled as his grandfather walked out of the kitchen with his Bible under his arm.

"Is he always this spry at four AM?" Josiah yawned, then sipped his coffee.

Michael smiled. "Pretty much. I take it you don't wake up at four in the city."

Josiah nearly laughed out loud. "Six is early enough to take care of my morning tasks and get to work on time."

"Must be nice."

"Ah...I kind of miss this."

"Really?" Sarcasm laced his tone. "Alright, what happened last night? You were gone for like two hours."

"It wasn't that long."

Michael eyed him with a smirk. "You like her, don't you?"

"Who, Miri?"

Michael wadded up a paper towel and threw it at him. "No, not my *fraa*. At least, you better not. And you know *exactly* who I'm referring to."

Josiah blew out a resigned breath. "Yes, I like her. A lot."

"Did you kiss her?"

Now it was Josiah's turn to throw the paper towel back at his friend. "No, of course, not."

"I would have."

"Does your *fraa* know this?" Josiah chuckled.

"I would if I were *you*."

"Yeah, well, at one point in time, you would have done a lot more than that."

Michael grimaced. "I wish I could erase that part of my life."

"We all have a past we wish we could erase." He shook his head. "I take that back. I bet Silas doesn't. He's as straight-laced as a pair of boots."

Michael's brow shot up. "You say that like it's a bad thing. What do you have against Silas?"

"Nothing."

"Doesn't sound like nothing."

"You know that one person who has a perfect life?"

"Silas's life is far from perfect. It sounds like there might be a little jealousy going on there."

"That might not be too far from the truth."

"Why?"

"You know."

"What? Because he married Kayla? He raised your daughter? I'd think you'd be happy about that. Or, at least thankful."

"Kayla chose him over me. And she had *my* daughter." He swallowed down his emotion.

"Ah, so *that's* what this is about." Michael nodded. "I see."

"I'm such an idiot."

"Hey, man, I've been there. Trust me on that. You're looking at the King of Idiocy right here." He aimed both of his pointing fingers at himself.

"I'm serious."

"So am I. But I discovered something, Joe. God couldn't help me *until* I got to that point in my life. And then, when I finally surrendered, my life totally changed. It was hard, man. Really hard. But I'm so glad I got to that point. Because if I hadn't, I'd still be an idiot. A fool."

"Look at us here. Just a couple of idiots sitting around drinking coffee." Josiah started laughing, then Mike joined in.

"Hey, what's the use if you can't laugh at yourself once in a while?" Michael covered his mouth. "Shh...we better shush before we wake up the *kinner*. Miri needs her sleep."

"What? You got another bun in the oven?"

Michael raised his eyebrows twice and grinned.

"Stud." Josiah chuckled.

"Don't I know it?" He flexed his muscles and they both burst into laughter again.

Michael suddenly stopped laughing. His eyes bored into Josiah's. "Seriously, Joe. Give it to God. He'll change your life."

Shivers ran up and down Bailey's arms. Today had to be the day. She knew it. She could feel it. She didn't know how or why, but she was sure and certain she'd get to meet her father today. She felt giddy from head-to-toe. Like she could run outside into the middle of the road and turn cartwheels.

She frowned. No, an Amish girl turning cartwheels in the middle of the road would not go over well with the leaders. But she felt like it anyhow. Would she do it if she was *Englisch*? What an absurd thought! But most of her thoughts had been that way lately, it seemed.

Jah, her father *had* to be coming today!

She stared at the clock. Eight fifteen. Ugh. Could this hour go by any slower?

The door jingled and she gasped.

"It's just me!" *Aendi* Jenny called out. "Will you get the rest of the baked goods from the buggy?"

"Sure." Anything to keep her mind occupied. She just hoped her aunt didn't plan on staying long. It wouldn't do to have her father show up while *Aenti* Jenny was here. She hurried out to the buggy and carried two trays inside. "Goodness, *Aenti* Jenny! Are you hoping for a rush today? I don't know if we'll sell all this."

Her aunt giggled. "Oh, I know. I couldn't help myself. I just got in a baking mood." She rubbed her hand over her large belly. "Must be this *boppli* coming soon. I always get this way when it's close to my time. And it's better to have it here than at home where your *Onkel* Paul will be stealing bites. Goodness, he's gained twenty pounds since we got married."

"That doesn't sound too bad. Haven't you been married seven years now?" She began helping her aunt arrange the baked goods in the glass display cases. The

95

sooner they could get this done, the sooner her aunt would leave the store. In theory, anyway.

"That's no excuse. But he's still handsome as ever."

She'd always thought her aunt and uncle made a cute couple. And her nieces and nephews were adorable. She wondered if this next *boppli* was a boy or a girl.

A bright flash reflected through the window. That seem to happen every time a vehicle pulled up and the sun was in a certain place. The fancy sportscar rolled to a stop.

It had to be her father! But *Aenti* Jenny was still here. She glanced at the clock. Nine o'clock already? How did that happen so fast? Yep, it was him. It had to be.

Okay. Just keep calm. Don't do anything foolish.

The door opened.

Ach, he was still as handsome as he'd been in the photos. Their eyes connected, then she glanced toward her aunt. He took the hint and nodded.

"We have a customer," she called to her aunt. "I can help him."

Her aunt seemed to pay no mind to him. And why would she? To her, he was just another *Englisch* customer.

"May I help you?" She stood behind the cash register.

"Yeah." His smile widened as they stared at each other, as though they shared a special secret between the two of them. But they *did* share a secret. And her aunt was oblivious to it. "I've heard this place has the best pot pies and cinnamon rolls in the area. Is that true?"

"That's what some have said." Bailey couldn't seem to wipe the smile off her face. She was having a conversation with her real *live* father!

"And where may I get some of these?" His voice was calm and gentle. Just how she'd expect her father's voice to be.

"My aunt Jenny can help you." Bailey gestured to the case her aunt was standing next to. Bailey couldn't get by if she tried. Not with her aunt's oversized midsection.

"Yes. I just brought them. They are fresh as fresh can be. Bailey and I placed them on the shelf not five minutes before you arrived." She placed her hand to her back. "How many would you like?"

"Let me get two of each, please."

Her aunt handed the items to her and she bagged them up for him. "Anything else?"

"That should do." He handed over the money after she'd given him the total. He moved his head ever so slightly to the side, indicating he wished to speak with her outside.

"Uh, *Aenti* Jenny. Will you keep an eye out for a minute? I need to go water the hanging flowers outside."

"Sure." Her aunt smiled.

Bailey held the door open for their customer, then followed him out with the water can in her hand.

"Bailey?"

"*Jah*." Her grin broadened. "I didn't know my aunt would show up. She usually comes earlier."

"I'd like to take you for ice cream. Is that a possibility?"

She filled the watering can with the hose, then began removing the hanging flower pots. "Um...*jah*. How about...can you meet me at the corner across the street from the stop sign down yonder at seven thirty tonight?" She pointed in the direction she was referring to.

"Sure thing, kid." He winked.

She planted her hand on her hip. "I'm hardly a kid anymore. I'm seventeen, you know."

"Forgive me. Young lady." He chuckled. "So much like your mother. I can see where you get your attitude from."

She began watering each of the plants. "Don't be late."

"Oh, I won't unless something happens. I better

get out of here before your aunt gets suspicious and comes out."

"Okay, then." Her smile dimmed a little. "Goodbye." *Dad.*

She watched as he slid into his fancy sportscar with his baked goods, then frowned as he drove away. It hadn't lasted long enough. They hadn't even had a chance to connect. But maybe they would tonight as they ate ice cream together.

TWELVE

Josiah squeezed the steering wheel. He'd seen his beautiful daughter! Sweetness and dynamite wrapped up in one package, it seemed. His smile must be stretching from ear to ear. Tonight couldn't come soon enough.

He inhaled the delicious scents filling his car. Instead of going straight to Michael's place to wait out his time, he'd stop by Nora's first. The extra cinnamon roll he'd purchased had been for her. And he could leave one of the pot pies for her too.

He pulled into her driveway and brought his vehicle to a stop. Nora stared curiously as she hung clothes on the line outside. He stepped out and waved. "Hey."

A look of recognition crossed her face and she finally smiled. She turned her head and he noticed that her two girls were swinging on a swing set nearby.

He approached with a bag in his hand. "I bring good tidings of great joy." He smiled. "Cinnamon rolls and pot pie."

"*Ach*, you didn't have to."

"I wanted to."

"Let's go inside, then? Unless you'd rather sit out back at the picnic table."

"That sounds good."

"Let me just grab a table cloth, then." She hurried to the house, then turned back. "Girls, show him where the picnic table is."

He wished he could remember what her daughters' names were. He followed them around the side of the house to the back yard. Like every house in this area, it seemed, the property was surrounded by a wooded area. It was breathtaking.

Nora walked out the back door carrying a colorful floral tablecloth, paper plates, and plasticware. "Sylvia and Esther didn't cause any trouble for you, did they?"

He doubted the two quiet little souls ever got into *any* trouble. "They were perfect angels."

"They usually are for the most part, but don't let them fool you." She squinted toward the girls. "Leave them alone with a closed box of cereal for a couple of minutes and you'll find it all over the floor. Huh, girls?"

Josiah grinned at the little ones. "Did you two have an adventurous morning?"

"If that's what you want to call it." Nora smiled.

He grasped one end of the tablecloth and they placed it over the table together. "What are their ages?"

"Sylvia is four and Esther is two and a half."

He frowned. "How long has Andy been gone?"

"Almost two years."

"That must've been hard for you."

"It was. But like I said, he was gone a lot." She shrugged. "Frankly, not much changed for me."

"Do you work outside the home now?"

"I do some. Andy left us a little money in our savings account, so I'm trying to make that stretch as far as I can." She spread the plates out on the table.

"I see."

"Are you hungry? It's still warm."

"I could eat."

"Good. Because the girls and I won't be able to eat all this by ourselves."

After they bowed for the silent prayer, she hopped up to get a serving utensil from the kitchen. She handed it to him. "Go ahead and serve yourself, then I'll serve the girls."

He refused the server and shook his head. "Ladies first. I insist."

"Okay." She smiled. "Girls, how much of this would you like?"

Neither one spoke.

"They seem to have gone mute. They're not used to strangers." She served each of her daughters a sliver, then placed a small portion on her own plate. "They don't eat much."

"It looks like their mother doesn't either." He eyed her plate. "I'm going to look like a pig."

The girls giggled.

"Oink oink." He snorted, evoking another round of giggles. He took a couple of bites then snorted again.

Nora laughed.

If he had to act like a pig to connect with these precious girls, he'd do so.

When they finally finished, they shared the cinnamon rolls. Again, he'd eaten the lion's share. "You were right. That cinnamon roll was really good."

"I just love them. Thank you, again, for bringing them. That was very thoughtful." She stood from the table. "I'm going to put the girls down for their naps. You want to come inside?"

He agreed because it seemed like that was her preference, likely to be in earshot of the girls.

"You may take a seat in the living room, if you'd like."

He did as she suggested as she guided the girls to their room. She returned a few moments later.

"How did your visit with your daughter go?" She sat in a recliner, across from where he sat on the couch.

"It didn't go as expected, but it was good. We're meeting for ice cream tonight." He smiled.

"What happened?"

"Her aunt was there. I guessed she'd just dropped off some baked goods, including those cinnamon rolls."

"Jenny is super sweet."

"You seemed to know the Millers pretty well."

She shrugged. "Oh, I hear quite a bit from Miriam. She and Michael and the *kinner* occasionally visit with the family, so I stay on top of things. I sometimes go along with Miriam when she purchases her baked goods. It seems like they do pretty well for a little country store. Between the bakery items and the metalwork that Silas and Paul make, along with their grocery and other miscellaneous items, I can see why."

"Metalwork?"

"*Jah*. Paul and Silas have a shop out back near their house. You probably saw the wind chimes hanging there outside the store." She smiled wistfully. "Don't they just sound lovely? The wind seems to lift their melodies on its wings and carry them away."

All of a sudden, he knew what one of his future purchases would be. Maybe he'd leave it with Elnora as a goodbye gift—a token of thanks for their friendship. Something about that thought didn't sit right with him.

"So, you and Kayla dated for a while, then?"

"Not really. Now that I look back on it, we hardly knew each other at all. It was a week at the beach. That's it. And, technically, it wasn't even a full week. We met, spent some time together, decided we were hopelessly in love with each other, then we shared that love. Or what we *thought* was love."

"Do you wish things would have turned out differently?"

He shrugged. "You know, that's one of those things. You can't really know that a different path would have been better. Do I have regrets? You bet I do. But I think the thing that irks me most is that I didn't make an effort to see my daughter. I missed all her growing up years.

"Even if I had found out that Kayla was pregnant, I'm not so sure I would have been that great of a husband to her. I was already wanting to leave all the constraints of Amish life behind. I don't know that I wouldn't have seen marriage to her as another limitation. I likely would have seen it as being tied down for life—a trap I couldn't get out of."

She frowned. "Do you still see it that way?"

"No, not at all. I was pretty immature back then. Your perspective changes once you've actually experienced life. Know what I mean?"

"For sure. I thought marriage was a fairytale. Before I actually experienced it. Then I realized that it's basically two people bringing their own problems to each other. And then you have to figure out a way to live with each other."

"But each person brings their own strengths to the relationship too, right?"

"Yes. You balance each other out." She looked toward the kitchen. "Would you like some lemonade?"

"That sounds great." Did he hear a noise in the other room? "How long do the girls usually sleep?"

She pulled a plastic pitcher out of the fridge. "Not long enough, usually." She smiled.

"I can see how naps could be priceless when you're solely responsible for little ones twenty-four hours a day, seven days a week."

"It sounds bad. I love them to pieces. But sometimes I just need quiet and solitude." She shook her head. "*Jah*, this morning when they decided they wanted to decorate the house with cereal, I had just gone to use the restroom. That was it. I return and suddenly I've got one more task to do for the day."

"It sounds like you need a break."

"You might be right."

"I have an idea. Why don't you bring the girls over to Michael and Miriam's one day, and you and Miriam can take a day off for yourselves. The guys can hold down the fort at home."

"Are you serious? Because don't say something like that if you're not serious."

"I'm completely serious. Of course, we'd have to schedule it with everybody first."

"Ah, Josiah, that sounds lovely." Tears pricked her eyes. "You would do that?"

"It wouldn't be a problem. I might even enlist Bailey to help out."

"She's likely a pro at it with all the younger siblings she has."

"Let's plan it, then! How about if we drive over there together once the girls wake up and share our idea with Miriam and Michael?"

"I would like that very much."

THIRTEEN

"He likes you, I know he does!" Miriam grasped Nora's arm and squealed the moment the men stepped outside. "I can't believe he came up with this plan. It's brilliant."

Nora shook her head. "We're just friends."

"Sounds like the perfect place to start a relationship." Miriam's grin stretched wide.

"He's *Englisch*." She reminded her overzealous matchmaking friend.

"That can change. His daughter is Amish, you're Amish, his friends are Amish."

Nora laughed. "You make it all sound so simple."

"It can be."

"Miriam, I can't ask him to give up his *Englisch* lifestyle for me. He'd come to resent me for it. It would have to be his decision—and his idea—totally."

"But you like him, right?"

"Oh, Miriam. What's not to like? *Jah*, he's made some dumb mistakes in the past. I think I can overlook that. But if you could just see." She shook her head. "The other night, when he brought the girls and me home, he carried little Esther to the bedroom. When he laid her down, he bent and kissed her cheek. He said he regretted not ever getting to do that with his own *dochder*." Moisture pricked her eyes.

"That's sweet. He sounds like a keeper."

"I just don't know if he's keepable."

"I'm not sure that's a word." Miriam giggled.

"Well, it is now."

Bailey did her best to slip out of the house and down the driveway unnoticed. She hadn't wanted to lie, so she left a note on the table saying she'd be back in a few hours. *Mamm* and Silas had taken the *kinner* over to *Dawdi* and *Mammi* Miller's for supper. Bailey made an excuse to stay behind. But getting out had been the easy part. Coming back in would prove to be tricky, apart from telling a lie, which she didn't wish to do.

She'd considered just telling her folks the truth in its entirety. But what if they weren't happy with her for contacting her father? What if they forbid her to see him? He was *Englisch*, after all. That alone would be excuse enough to keep him away from her. And then he would have come all this way for no reason. She was sure he'd probably spent hundreds of dollars coming all the way over here from Pennsylvania.

She didn't like sneaking around, but if that was the only way she could see her father, she'd do it. She kind of liked the fact that she and her father shared a secret, though.

She hurried out to the end of the driveway, making her way toward the stop sign up ahead. It was right around the time she'd told her father she'd meet him. She couldn't be late. Her lips curled into a smile when she spotted her father's fancy sportscar across the road from the stop sign.

She quickly looked behind her to be sure no one was on the road. It wouldn't do to be seen by someone in the community.

The moment her father spotted her, he began creeping forward. He pulled up beside her and rolled down the window. "Hey, pretty girl. Are you looking for a ride?" He winked.

Ach, no wonder *Mamm* had fallen in love with him back in the day. "I don't know. My folks always told me not to accept rides from strangers." She bantered, as she opened the car door and slid into the seat. She immediately smelled leather.

"I'm harmless. I promise." He flipped a U-turn, then came to a stop at the stop sign. He pulled out onto the main road. "Does Dairy Queen sound all right?"

"Sure, that's fine."

"Do you have a favorite kind of ice cream?"

"You mean at DQ or in general?"

He shrugged. "Either. Both."

"I like their cotton candy ice cream cones."

"Cotton candy?" His brow arched. "I've never tried it. It sounds really sweet, though."

"It is." She studied him. "Do you have a favorite?"

"I like anything chocolate. The more chocolate the better. And I like peanut butter milkshakes. And hot fudge sundaes, and caramel sundaes, and—"

"I think I get the picture, *Dad*." She frowned. "Is it okay if I call you that?"

"I'd love it if you call me that."

"Okay, *That*." She teased.

"How'd you get so spunky?" He reached over and tweaked her nose.

"Spunky?" She giggled. "I don't know. I guess I was born with it."

"So...how can we get to know each other? To make up for all these years we've lost?"

"We could play a get-to-know-you game."

"And how do you play that or I should say the get-to-know-you game?"

"Well, it's simple. We just take turns asking each other questions."

"Sounds easy enough." He nodded. "Okay, you start, since I already asked you about ice cream."

"Okay. Let me think. Where do you live?"

"I live in New Jersey."

"Not Pennsylvania?"

"Ah, that's two questions. And no, not Pennsylvania." He grinned. "Okay, my turn. Where were you born?"

"In California. Do you live by yourself?"

"No, I have a cat named Maestro."

"Really? *You* have a cat?"

"That's two questions again."

She ignored his protest. "I like cats too."

"Do you have any?"

"Yes, Sandy. But he's getting old. Are you married?"

"No. Never been. Are you?" he winked.

"No, silly."

"Boyfriend?"

She pointed at him. "That's two questions. And sort-of."

"How can you sort-of have a boyfriend?"

"That's three questions. Not fair." She blew out a breath. "Timothy and I are a long story. His folks don't want him to date me because they think I'll jump the fence because I used to be *Englisch*."

"Will you?"

She shrugged. "I never thought I would."

"It's not that bad."

She stared at him. "But you're like forty and you live alone."

"Ouch! Hey, I'm not forty yet. Thirty-seven."

"It's almost the same thing."

He chuckled. "You're rough, girl."

"I speak the truth. Aren't you lonely? I'd be lonely all by myself with no family around."

"Honestly, sometimes, yes." He sighed.

They pulled into the Dairy Queen parking area. "Do you want to eat outside or should we get it to go and find a park or something?"

"We could go to Versailles State Park. I think there will be less chances of people seeing us there."

"That sounds nice. What would you like?" He smiled as they were parked in front of the ordering menu.

"A cotton candy cone." She grinned.

"Two cotton candy cones," he spoke into the speaker.

"And may I get french fries?"

"And an order of french fries," he called out. The server told him the total, and he inched forward. He turned to her. "Do they have a picnic area at the park?"

"*Jah*. And a covered bridge."

"Really?"

"Timothy brought me one time."

"Oh?"

She wouldn't tell him that was the first time he'd kissed her.

Dad paid for their order, then handed Bailey her ice cream cone and fries.

Her smile widened. "I like to dip the French fries in my ice cream."

His lips twisted.

She handed him a fry. "Here, try it."

He took the french fry and did as she directed. "Mmm...hey, that's not bad."

"I like the sweet and salty together."

"It's good. But it might be difficult to eat it that way while driving."

"You're right."

"You'll have to show me how to get there, unless you'd rather I use GPS. I think it'll work here since we're not out in the boonies."

"It's easy to find. Just turn right at the light up there. Then you follow the road. I think it's just a couple of miles. You'll see the signs."

"Sounds easy enough."

She dipped a fry into her ice cream and popped it into her mouth. "This is so good. Thank you."

"I've got a lot to make up for."

"You don't have to buy me anything. I just want to spend time with you."

He reached over and squeezed her hand. "You don't know how happy that makes my heart."

"I feel the same way. I'm just glad that I can finally know you. I've missed you all these years, but I thought you were dead. So, you being here is kind of like having you back from the dead." She wouldn't cry. She blinked her eyes to avoid tears. She. Would. Not. Cry.

"Here we are." He turned left into the park entrance. "Do we turn at the covered bridge?"

"No, just go straight. If you want, we could go through the covered bridge on the way back. It goes back into Versailles."

"Okay." He pulled up to the kiosk and paid the small day use fee. He continued down the road. "It's pretty here."

"I know. I love it. It would be fun to camp out."

"Have you ever?"

"No."

"We should, then. I'm sure my friends would love to join us."

"Your friends?"

"You might know them. Michael and Miriam Eicher. And Elnora Schwartz."

"Yes, I know them." She nodded, then pointed up ahead. "It's right there."

He pulled into the small lot near a picnic area and they got out of the car. "I'm staying with the Eichers."

"I didn't know that. Michael is a friend of Silas's too."

He grimaced. "*Jah*, Michael and I have been friends for a long time. Your dad—well, Silas—was part of our group of friends, along with a couple others. Michael and I kept in touch. He's probably the only one who knew I wasn't dead from day one. We were both pretty worldly back then."

"But you didn't keep in touch with Silas?" She sat on the picnic bench, across from her father.

"No. I didn't think he'd be able to keep my secret. He was just so...honest. I know, that sounds wrong. It's a good thing to be honest. Silas has always been a better person than I could ever be."

"Anyone can be good." Her voice escaped as a whisper.

"I know. But I wasn't. Not then."

"But you are now?"

He shrugged. "I'm trying."

She stopped licking her ice cream and stared at him. "May I ask you a question, Dad?"

"Sure. Anything."

"Do you know Jesus?"

"What do you mean by that?"

"I mean, does He live in your heart? Did you ever invite Him inside?"

He frowned. "That doesn't sound very Amish to me."

"It's in the Bible. I'm not sure where, but *Mamm* and Silas read it to me before."

"Hm...no, I can't say that I have."

"Because Silas said that's what makes a person good—Jesus. He comes inside your heart and makes you a good person."

He smiled. "That's an interesting concept."

"Will you invite Jesus into your heart?"

He held up his hands and shook his head. "I don't embrace anything without first studying the validity of it."

She twisted her lips. "What do you mean?"

"I want to know what I believe. There has to be a reason behind it."

"Oh, that's easy. It's so we can go to Heaven and live forever with God."

"Like I said, I'll have to study that."

"But will you, for real? Or are you just saying that?" She challenged. "Because if you really mean it, I can help you find the verses. I can ask Silas. He's very smart about the Bible." A sense of pride washed over her as she said the words.

"Silas is a good man." He blew out a long breath. "I could never measure up."

"You don't have to. I love you just the way you are."

He studied her carefully. "Do you mean that?"

"With all my heart."

He moved to her side of the table and opened his arms. She melted into her father's embrace. "I love you too, Bailey." His voice sounded shaky to her ears. When she finally pulled back, there were tears in his eyes.

"You know, this just might be the best day of my life." He pressed his lips to the side of her prayer *kapp*.

Bailey decided it was definitely one of hers too.

FOURTEEN

Josiah dropped Bailey off just beyond the end of the Millers' long driveway, then waited back until she was safely inside her home. He still couldn't get over how well his reunion with his daughter had gone. He hadn't been in the habit of talking to God, but if there ever was any time to give thanks, it was tonight.

He was a blessed man. A blessed *father*. And he knew he didn't deserve any of it.

He couldn't wait to share his news with Nora. She'd told him that she'd be praying. God must've heard her prayers.

He didn't know what he'd been expecting to happen with Bailey, but tonight had exceeded any scenario his mind could have conjured up. He actually had a *real* relationship with his daughter. From this point on, both of their lives would change.

Bailey slipped through the door and attempted to tiptoe to her room unseen.

"Bailey? Is that you? Are you home?" It was *Mamm*.

Busted. "*Jah*, I'm home now."

"Come sit at the table with *Dat* and me," *Mamm* called.

She sighed, then did as bidden.

"You were out late," Silas said.

"Not really. It's only ten."

"It's later than usual for a night when there is no young folks' gathering. Where were you?"

"I went out for ice cream."

Her parents looked at each other.

"Ice cream? Who were you with?"

"I'd rather not say." She stared at the floor. Then her hands. Anywhere but at her folks.

"Bailey." Silas sighed. "You and Timothy are not supposed to be seeing each other."

"I know." She'd let them believe it was Timothy. She wouldn't say who it was unless she was asked directly.

"Do you remember what we talked about the other night? Bailey, we're trying to guide you the best way we know how, but if you go against our advice..." Silas frowned. "We just don't want to see you hurt."

"I know." Maybe if she changed the subject, her folks would direct their thoughts elsewhere. It was worth a shot anyway. "*Dat*, remember when we were talking about having Jesus in your heart? And you said that when Jesus comes into your heart, He makes you good?"

"*Jah*. You have the righteousness of Christ." He glanced at *Mamm* and smiled slightly.

"That's in the Bible, right?"

"It is."

"Could you maybe show me where?"

"Certainly." He nodded. "Let's go into the living room and sit on the couch. My Bible is on the table in there. Why don't you get yours too, and maybe a pen and notebook?"

"Okay." She rushed to her room, happy that she hadn't only distracted her folks from her tardiness, but that she would be getting something she could share with her father. She hurried back into the living room and joined her folks on the sofa.

Silas grinned. Bailey loved that her stepfather loved studying the Bible. Any time she needed answers, she could go to him and he usually knew. If he didn't, they would study together until they found the answers they were looking for.

"Let's just start with these verses, which talk about

Jesus dwelling inside of believers." He looked up from his Bible. "First John 4:4. I'll just read the second part."

She wrote down the reference and poised her pen to write the words he'd read.

"Greater is he that is in you, than he that is in the world."

"*Ach*, I like that one." She smiled.

"Revelation 3:20. Behold, I stand at the door, and knock; if any man hear my voice, and open the door, I will come in to him, and will sup with him, and he with me."

She hurried to jot it all down in her notebook.

"And I'm going to let you look these other ones up on your own, but I'll give you the references. Romans chapter eight, the whole chapter is awesome. Romans 3:22 talks about having God's righteousness. So does Philippians 3:9. Second Corinthians 13:5. Ephesians 3:17. Colossians 1:27. And I'm sure there are others, but that's plenty for now."

She couldn't wait to look all these up and share them with Dad.

Nora had a feeling Josiah would be stopping by this evening. She'd purposely stayed up later than usual tonight. The girls had already been sleeping a few hours. She checked the clock again, then decided she'd put on some water for tea. She didn't need coffee. That would keep her alert until morning and then she'd be worthless tomorrow.

Her heart did a somersault the moment she saw the vehicle's lights flash on the wall through the curtain. *He's here.*

She pulled a sweater from the hook near the door and stepped out into the balmy air. Josiah hastened his steps toward the house, toward her. Instead of greeting her with a hello, he practically sprinted toward her, then lifted her off the ground, spun her once, and let her down again.

She caught her breath. "Goodness, I'm guessing it went well then?"

He stepped back, his eyes sparkling. He leaned forward and embraced her again, then pressed his lips to her cheek. "*Denki* for praying. *Ach*, it went *wunderbaar!*"

"You're slipping back into *Deitch*, you realize that, don't you?" She laughed. "I'm happy it went well."

"Better than I ever imagined, Nora! We talked, we connected, we hugged each other and said 'I love you.' It was probably the best day of my life." His eyes moistened.

"Wow, Josiah. That really is *wunderbaar!*"

"Let's go inside?"

"Yes." She opened the door and he followed her inside. "I put on some water, if you'd like a cup of tea."

"That sounds perfect."

"Do you like peppermint?"

"I love peppermint. That's what my mom would make all the time back in the day."

"So, what are you going to do now? What's the next step?" She gestured for him to take a seat at the dining table.

"Bailey wants to spend time with me so we can get to know each other better." He practically radiated light, he was so vibrant.

"That's great. I bet you're happy about that."

"I'm ecstatic. I didn't even know if she'd want to see me. Or I thought maybe she'd chew me out like her mom did."

Nora gasped. "Kayla chewed you out?"

"In a manner of speaking, yes. But I can't blame her." He shook his head. "She thought I was dead, then all of a sudden she receives a letter from me a week before she's about to marry Silas. I don't know what I was thinking."

"What did your letter say?"

"Just that I was alive and I found out that we had a

child and if she didn't want to become Amish that I would help her raise our child. I was too late."

"I'm sorry."

He shrugged. "I guess things happen the way they do for a reason. I just wish I wouldn't have given up my daughter so easily."

"It seems like Bailey is pretty understanding." She removed two mugs from the cupboard and slid one to him, along with a tea bag.

He nodded his thanks. "Yes. And forgiving. Ah, she's such a great girl. I missed out on so much, not knowing her."

"Well, there's no sense dwelling on should-haves and would-haves. You start right here, right now, and you make the best of it." She poured water into each of their mugs, placed a saucer over them to steep, then finally placed the honey and a spoon on the table, and sat down.

He reached for her hand. "I love that you're so practical."

She'd take his declaration as a compliment. Practicality was a good thing, right? "What do you plan to do now?"

"Just spend time with my daughter, I guess. I told her that we probably need to let her parents know that I'm here. Sooner rather than later. I don't like that she's going behind their backs."

She tried to ignore the delightful sensation that filled her as her hand rested in his. He didn't mean anything by it, so she shouldn't read anything into it. Just like she shouldn't read anything into how he'd embraced her and spun her around and grazed her cheek with a kiss. It was just excitement on his part, adrenaline from his time with his *dochder*. Plain and simple. "Are you going to visit them?"

"Since Bailey's the one who contacted me, I'm kind of letting her take the wheel. She'll tell them when she's ready."

"You realized that once that all happens, word will get out that you're still alive. You won't be able to hide anymore."

"Yeah, I know. I should probably make a trip to Pennsylvania before too long. It would be better if my parents heard it straight from me." He released a heavy sigh.

"That sounds like it might be a difficult task for you."

"No doubt about that. I mean, I can only imagine how my parents are going to react after thinking I've been dead for the past eighteen years. But if that's what I need to do to have Bailey in my life, then I'll do what it takes."

"I'll be praying for you."

"Thank you, Nora." He brought her hand to his lips and kissed her fingers. "I'm certain it was your prayers that paved the way for my time with Bailey this evening. You seem to have a connection."

She shook her head. "No more than anyone else. Doesn't God answer your prayers?"

"I don't...I haven't *really* prayed in a long, long time."

She gasped, instinctually pulling her hand away. She grasped for the honey, to recover. "*Ach*, I...I don't know what to say to that."

"When I left the Amish, I left all that behind me, including the religious part." He clasped his hands together on top of the table.

"I can't even imagine not talking to *Der Herr* throughout the day, not thanking Him for the blessings He bestows on me every day." Sadness washed over her.

"Bailey tried to talk to me about the Bible tonight." He smiled, but it morphed into a grimace. "It looks like Silas has done his job well."

A thought occurred to her. "You didn't try to sway her against it, did you? Because Jesus said it is better for a millstone to be tied around a person's neck and that they be cast in the sea than to offend the little ones."

"No, I wouldn't do that. At least, I don't think I would." He took the plastic honey bear she offered and added a little to his tea, stirring the hot beverage to dissolve the honey. "I just told her that I like to study things out before I embrace them as truth."

"Is that true?"

"*Jah*, why?" He sipped his tea.

She shrugged. "You do that with everything?"

He chuckled. "Pretty much. I'm a huge skeptic. I think one has to be in this day with so many scammers and liars out there."

"You make a *gut* point." And she was okay with that, she realized. Didn't *Der Herr* say that if one sought after Him they would find Him, if they searched with all their heart? *Gott, please show Yourself to Josiah.* Maybe He already was.

He pulled out his cell phone and stared at it. "Bailey's supposed to call me when she wants to meet up next. Judging by her enthusiasm tonight, it probably won't be too long."

"You don't think she'll be calling tonight, do you?"

"Nah, just wishful thinking, I guess." He chuckled. "Until then, I'm all Sammy's. I'm sure he has plenty of projects for me to do around the farm."

"You know he does."

He drained his tea in one gulp. "I should let you get

some rest before the little angels awaken."

She smiled. "They sure do look that way when they're sleeping."

He stood. "Thank you for everything. The tea, the conversation. It's nice having a listening ear."

"I enjoy our time together." She followed him to the door.

He stopped and turned to her. "Yeah, me too." His hand moved to caress her earlobe, then his fingers slid down her *kapp* string. "Nora..." His eyes flashed with something. Longing, maybe?

She dipped her head slightly, then lifted her gaze to his.

"I might—" He ceased talking when his arm slipped around her waist, his other hand was at the back of her *kapp*. He leaned down, but he didn't kiss her cheek this time. No, his mouth went straight to her lips, moving ever so gently over them.

She grasped a fistful of his shirt, pulling him taut against her. Her fingers tantalized the hair at the nape of his neck, as she tilted her head slightly and he deepened the kiss. His hands massaged her neck, moving down her back, pressing her to him, then moved to her *kapp*, feeling for the straight pin that held it in place.

She felt her hair tumble down her back and around

her shoulders, his fingers entangled in it.

His mouth moved to her jawline, her earlobe, her neck. "Nora..." His breath was heavy, his gaze dreamy. "We can't...we shouldn't..." His mouth returned to hers.

She realized that if she didn't force herself away, Josiah might not be returning to the Eichers' tonight. *Ach*, but she'd missed being married. Having strong arms holding her close at night, or anytime, for that matter. She missed the excitement, letting passion roam where it willed. She missed the companionship of a husband.

But Josiah was *not* her husband, although he was behaving very much as a husband would with his *fraa*. As a matter of fact, Josiah was an *Englischer*, who never even expressed an interest in becoming Plain again. What on earth was she doing? This would only lead to heartache.

"Josiah, no." She finally broke away. "We can't do this. You're not even—you're *Englisch*."

His hair was disheveled along with his clothes. He moved back but desire burned in his eyes. "I want you, Nora." His voice came out husky.

"Then marry me," she whispered.

He released her completely. Like he'd grabbed a hot potato and burned himself.

Tears shimmered in her eyes. She already knew what his answer would be. She'd been fooling herself to think that they could actually have something real and lasting.

He shook his head. "I can't." He balled his hands into fists. "I'm sorry, Nora. We never should have..." He squeezed his eyes shut. "I should go."

Nora watched in dismay as he practically ran out the door to his car. Like he couldn't get out of her presence quickly enough.

It wasn't until he'd zoomed down the road, until the lights from his vehicle faded from view, until the dust had cleared, that she allowed her tears to fall freely.

Way to go, Josiah. He was an idiot, plain and simple. How many times had he told himself he was *not* going to kiss her? Was. Not. And then he went and did it. And it was way worse than he ever imagined. Or, to be more accurate, way *better* than he ever imagined.

And now...what on earth was he going to do? She wanted marriage. She *expected* marriage—and she *should*. An amazing woman like Nora deserved to be loved fully and completely. But he wasn't the right person. He wasn't even Amish. And he didn't even know if he *could* be Amish again. Because becoming Amish again would mean he'd have to agree to submit to the gazillion rules of the Amish church that had no rhyme or reason. Exactly what he fought so hard to get away from. He wasn't going back.

Maybe it had been a mistake to come here. Not the part about meeting his daughter, of course, but jumping into the Amish world by living with the Eichers. He had to leave. Maybe get a motel room or something—probably what he should have done in the first place.

Or maybe he should just go back home. But he didn't want to leave Bailey. Again. He couldn't.

Instead of driving back to Michael's, he decided to search for a motel on his cell phone. It was late, but he'd still be able to get a room. He found one that seemed decent, called the number, and made a quick reservation. He'd sleep there, at least for tonight. He'd figure the rest out in the morning.

FIFTEEN

Josiah awakened to the buzzing of his phone. It was Michael. "Hey."

"Where are you? Did you spend the night at Nora's?"

"What? No." Not that he hadn't *wanted* to.

"Are you still asleep, man?"

He yawned and wiped the crustiness from his eyes. "I *was*. What time is it?"

"Almost nine."

"You're kidding." He pulled his phone away to look at the time, but remembered he was on a call. He glanced at the alarm clock. Eight forty-five. Hopefully, he hadn't missed the continental breakfast.

"Where'd you stay the night?"

"I got a hotel."

"Why? Why pay when you can stay here for free?"

"It's complicated."

"Oh, no. Nora?"

"Yeah, something like that."

"So, can we expect you out at the farm today?"

"I haven't decided what my plans are just yet. But I should wash those clothes and get them back to Nora." He could stop by when he knew she'd be gone. He'd leave them on her picnic table in a bag with a note expressing his gratitude for the use of them. And maybe some sort of farewell.

"Are you leaving, man?"

"I don't know. I'm not sure."

"What about your daughter?"

"We had a wonderful visit yesterday. I need to talk to her again. She'd said she'd call me when she could, so I'll probably be waiting around for her call."

"Well, I'm glad to hear it went well. Just, if you leave, make sure to stop by and say goodbye to everyone, will ya?"

"Yeah, sure."

They said their goodbyes.

Josiah reached for the motel information card. Breakfast was available until nine. Perfect. He'd run down to the dining area and grab a bite to eat before he headed out for the day.

He thought about his daughter. Leaving her was going to be difficult for both of them. But he couldn't stay here forever anyhow. He had a job to get back to. He briefly wondered if Bailey would be willing to let him snap a few pictures of the two of them together. A smile crept across his face at the thought of framing them and placing them on his desk at work.

He'd spied some shops last night when he pulled in, and he was pretty certain they were within walking distance. If he decided to go back home, he wanted to leave something with Bailey. Something special.

Several moments later, he perused the jewelry in one of the small department stores. His eyes zeroed in on a silver pendant with the word Daughter on it. This necklace would be perfect. He didn't expect Bailey to wear the token of his love, but he hoped she'd count it among her treasures.

Truly, he wanted to stay longer. He and Bailey *needed* more time together. But a hundred dollars a night wasn't exactly cheap, even with biscuits and gravy in the morning. He could still stay with Michael. It wasn't as if he'd been asked to leave. But he feared he'd run into Nora. He couldn't make any commitments or attachments here—two things he'd never been good at.

Thankfully, when Josiah pulled up to the farm, Nora's buggy was absent. If she believed he was there, there was a good chance she'd be staying away until he'd left for good. The thought pained him more then he wanted to admit. He cared deeply for Nora and he'd grown fond of her girls. He'd even entertained a thought or two of the four of them becoming a family.

But he didn't do families. He was a one-man show.

Michael met him as he stepped out of the car. "You came back. Good. I think *Dawdi* wants to put you to work already." He chuckled. "Unless you have other plans for today?"

"No, not yet. Unless I get a call from Bailey, I'm all Sammy's."

"Well, better suit up, then. The day is a-wastin'." Michael pounded his back.

As they approached the house, Michael's wife and children descended from the porch. "Isn't she just a sight for sore eyes." He growled like a feral cat.

"Oh, stop." Miriam laughed and playfully pushed her husband's arm.

Michael pulled her near and planted a kiss on her neck.

Josiah stood by awkwardly, averting his gaze yet enjoying their playfulness. Would he ever have that kind of relationship with a woman? *Nora.*

"*Ach*, not with Josiah here." She squirmed under his touch.

"Then kiss me goodbye, at least."

"I'd think you got enough kissing this morning," Josiah overheard her whisper in Michael's ear, as her brow arched high.

"Mm...there's no such thing as enough, *fraa*." He leaned down and kissed her, then reluctantly released her, watching longingly as she made her way to the buggy where the children waited with Sammy.

"Mm...mm." Michael shook his head. "I don't think I'll ever get enough of that woman. What she does to me..."

Josiah chuckled as they finally made their way into the house. "Well, it looks like you married the right one."

"Don't I know it." He couldn't seem to hide his mischievous grin. "When are you finally going to settle down?"

"Family life isn't for me, man."

"Why not?"

"I don't know. I don't think I can handle it all. A wife. Kids."

"Oh, I can't either."

"What do you mean?"

"Not without God. He gives me the strength I need for each day."

"How so?"

"I read His Word. Check this out. *Husbands, love your wives as Christ loved the church.*" He quoted. "That verse knocks me out every single time. Think about it. Christ sacrificed everything, including His very life, for the church. That means every single day I have to die to myself and put her needs above my own."

"It sounds hard."

"*Jah*, but I love her. When you love someone, you want to serve them, to make them happy, to supply their needs. Kind of like what you said you wanted to do for Nora."

"What did I say I wanted to do for Nora?"

"To give her the day off and watch the *kinner*. Have you forgotten already?"

He slapped a palm to his forehead. "See? That's exactly what I mean. I'm not good at this."

"You learn as you go along. You'll make mistakes, everyone does. You'll get upset and angry with each other. That's normal. But once you work through it, you're stronger." Michael squeezed his arm and lifted a lopsided grin. "And then you get to kiss and make up."

"Why am I thinking you cause problems on purpose just so you can get to the end result?"

Michael lifted a finger to his lips. "Shh...it's our little secret."

Josiah laughed out loud.

"You know, there's something to be said for friends and family and community. They help keep your feet on the right path."

"I don't know. Truthfully, I'm afraid of myself. I mean, what if I *did* convert and marry Nora, and then it's too much and I skip town? I've already left enough disappointment and broken hearts in my wake. Look at Kayla and Bailey."

"You might see it that way, but I think you'd be surprised that Kayla doesn't. She found God because of your mistakes. She found Silas because of your mistakes. She found a community and purpose for her life because of your mistakes."

"No, it was *in spite* of my mistakes."

"Either way, God took it and He used it for good."

"I don't know how to make it all work."

"The key is handing over the pieces to the Master Puzzle-Solver and allowing *Him* to make it work."

"I just see in my mind these two paths. One is easy. It goes straight back to New Jersey, back to my high-paying job, back to the life I've known for the past decade. The other one, well, it's quite different. It's difficult. It's full of pain and trials and unknowns. *Why* would I *choose* the difficult path?"

"How do you know it's difficult?"

"Because. You know, until Bailey's letter came for me, I don't think I'd ever really cried. And now? Sheesh! I'm bawling like a baby at every turn. No matter if it's Bailey or Nora."

"It sounds like you've finally started living."

Josiah frowned. "I don't know. I'm not used to all this...emotion."

"And you think your life would be *better* if Bailey and Nora weren't in it? I hate to tell you this, Joe, but you're already here. You've already stepped into their lives. If you leave now, neither your life, nor theirs will ever be the same. If you think that you can just go back to New Jersey and carry on as you always have, you are sorely mistaken. Allow yourself to love, Joe. Ignore the 'what ifs?' and live your life."

"You make it sound so easy."

"I don't know about easy, but I don't think it's as complicated as you think it is. Maybe you need to spend some time in prayer."

Prayer. *Right*. Why did it seem like everyone had this praying thing down, except him?

Sammy's voice hollered through the house. "You two gonna be yakking in here all day or are we gonna get that hay moved?"

"We're coming, *Dawdi*." Michael motioned to the door.

Sammy snapped his fingers. "Let's snap to it! I'm worried your jaw muscles are going to pass up them big arm muscles you young folks seem to be so fond of."

Michael laughed. "I spent quite a few years at the gym getting them to look this way, *Dawdi*."

Sammy sneered. "Waste of time, if you ask me."

"I think my *fraa* might disagree with you there, *Dawdi*." He glanced at Josiah and raised his eyebrows. "She likes them."

Sammy grunted.

SIXTEEN

Bailey had a plan. It was a brilliant one, if she did say so herself. Now, if she could just put everything into motion and if everything would fall in line, it would be great. At least, she hoped it would.

As soon as the coast was clear, she headed for the phone shanty. Fortunately, Dad picked up on the first ring, which made her smile. Like he'd been anticipating her call.

"How's the most beautiful girl in the world doing?"

Ach, his words made her cheeks heat. She wasn't used to the way *Englischers* spoke with so much vanity. "*Dad...*"

"I know, I know. It's not the Amish way. But it is the truth."

"Stop, already, Dad."

"Okay. What's up, Bay?"

"Bay?"

"Nickname. Do you like it? Or I could call you George."

She frowned. "George? Why would you call me a boy's name?"

He chuckled. "George Bailey. It's a character from a very famous Christmas movie called, *It's A Wonderful Life*."

"A movie, Dad? Really?"

"It's a good movie. Maybe I'll download it on my laptop and we can make some popcorn and watch it. Would you like that?"

"That sounds like fun, but I don't know when we could do it."

"You give me a time and I'll figure out the logistics."

"The what? Never mind. Okay, I better hurry because I don't want *Mamm* or Silas getting suspicious."

"Do you always call him Silas?"

"No. I mean, I guess I do *now* sometimes. Since I found your letter and I knew you were still alive. You're my dad."

Dad's breath seemed a little heavy over the phone, but he didn't respond.

"Are you still there, Dad?"

"Yeah, yeah. I just, I'm getting used to this dad thing. I'm a little emotional about it."

"You're so adorable."

He chuckled.

"Okay, back on track before I have to go. Can you meet me at ten o'clock at DQ tomorrow morning?"

"Meet you there? Yeah, sure. You want more ice cream?"

"I just want to see you. Maybe we'll end up going somewhere else like last time."

"You have a ride?"

"Yes."

"Okay, I'll see you there at ten o'clock then."

"Kay. Bye." Bailey hung up the phone and smiled. So far, everything was going exactly according to plan.

Josiah rolled up to the Dairy Queen parking lot at five till ten. He didn't want Bailey waiting around long for him in case she was early. He decided to just lay low inside the car in case her driver saw him. He didn't want anyone thinking anything suspicious was going on.

A couple of minutes later, he glanced in his review mirror and spotted not one, but two Amish women walking toward Dairy Queen from the IGA parking lot. Did she bring a friend along to meet him? Maybe he should just stay in the car in case Bailey had in mind to send her friend away. He'd wait and let her make the first move.

Just as he thought, she and her friend walked right past his vehicle and up to the order counter. Bailey stood behind the other girl, who was now ordering. His daughter turned to him and waved him over while the other girl was placing her order. She must want to introduce him to her friend.

He stepped out of the car and walked toward the window. The other girl finished ordering, then turned around. Except it wasn't another girl at all. It was a woman. *Kayla*.

He swallowed and stared at her. Her mouth dropped open as her eyes registered recognition. They both turned to Bailey.

Bailey smiled tentatively, her gaze bouncing back and forth to each of them. "Surprise."

Kayla frowned. "Bailey. It's...what...*Josiah*?"

"In the flesh." He tried to smile, but it faltered. He wasn't prepared for this.

"What are you doing here? *Why* are you here?" Kayla didn't look happy.

"He came to see me, *Mamm*," Bailey chimed in.

148

"I got a letter from our daughter a couple of weeks ago. She wanted to see me and I wanted to see her, so I came," he explained.

"Don't be mad, *Mamm*. Please. I brought you here because I wanted you two to talk."

Josiah and Kayla looked at each other, then at Bailey. "Talk?"

"Yeah. About the past. I mean, you need to. You have to work things out." Bailey looked around. "Maybe we should go somewhere else, since people are coming."

"Yes, we should." He agreed when he noticed that a couple of people had taken an interest in them.

Bailey quickly retrieved their food from the takeout window.

Josiah urged Kayla to walk to his car, but she shook her head. "Our driver's coming to pick us up in a half hour."

Bailey came up beside her, handing her mother her order. "*Nee*, *Mamm*. I told them we already had a ride back home."

Kayla gasped. "When did you tell them that?"

"When you were walking into the store. Remember I ran back for my purse?" She was sneaky.

Kayla rolled her eyes.

They all slid into his car. Bailey in the back, Kayla

in the passenger's seat. He pulled out onto the road and began driving toward the same place he and Bailey had gone last time, because he didn't know of anywhere else to go.

"We could go to the library," Bailey suggested.

"Libraries are supposed to be quiet. And I'm not sure how quiet this conversation is going to be," Josiah mumbled. *Oh, boy.*

"Bailey, you deceived me. Both of us. You tricked us into coming here. That's not right." Her mother frowned. It seemed about the only expression she had when he was around.

"Kayla, it's okay," he said, attempting to save his daughter from a reprimand.

She spun to face him and pointed a finger in his chest. "No, it's not okay! I don't want my daughter to grow up to be a deceiver just like her father was. *Is.*"

He frowned. "That's low."

"It's the truth, Josiah! Does your family still think you're dead?"

He hung his head, working his jaw. "Yes. But Bailey's a sweet girl. You raised her well."

"No thanks to you," she spat out.

"*Me*? As I recall, *I* offered to help you raise *our* daughter. *You* chose Silas!"

"Don't even..." She shook her head. "Josiah, I

thought you were dead until a week before my wedding! What did you expect me to do?"

He rubbed his forehead. "I don't know. Maybe remember that we once loved each other enough to make a child together. Maybe postpone your wedding to see if we could make it work between us."

"That's not fair. I loved Silas. And I could *never* have done that to him. You *don't* just walk away from the people you love, Josiah! Or maybe you haven't figured that out yet."

Her comment hit its mark squarely in the bullseye.

"*Mamm*," Bailey squeaked from the back seat.

She twisted in her seat. "You wanted us to talk, Bailey. That's what we're doing."

Josiah peeked at the rearview mirror just in time to see his daughter wipe away a tear. He parked across the street from the library, but they stayed inside the car.

"I want you to be nice to each other!" Bailey cried. "I love Dad! I want him in my life."

Kayla's lips formed a hard line.

"Kayla," he said in the most gentle voice he could muster. He dared to reach over and touch her hand. "Will you forgive me?"

She yanked her hand away. "I don't know if I can."

"Why?"

"Here, I was sixteen. And—"

"You were *sixteen*?"

"Yes. I know. I told you that I was older because I thought *you* were older."

"I was."

She continued, "I was sixteen. And pregnant. And alone. And then I find out that *you*—you left *everything* because you just *wanted* to go out and have a *good time* and do whatever the heck you pleased!"

"*Mamm*!"

"I'm sorry, Bailey. I'm mad. Sometimes people say things they shouldn't when they're mad. I know, it's no excuse. But your father seems to bring out the worst in me."

"Don't say that, *Mamm*!"

He hated that Bailey had to be a witness to this conversation. He didn't blame Kayla for being upset. He deserved her harsh words—and more. But he didn't have a clue how to make this right. Making things right with Bailey had been a breeze in comparison to her mother.

He sighed. "What do you want me to do? Tell me. I'll do it."

"Go back home or to *wherever* you came from."

"*Mamm*, no! He's my dad! I don't want him to *ever* go back."

Bailey's words warmed his heart. But maybe Kayla was right. Maybe he never should have come. Maybe it would have been less traumatic for Bailey if he had never come in the first place. But like Michael had said, he was *already* here. And because of that, none of their lives would ever be the same again.

"Is that what you really want, Kayla? For me to go and never come back?"

"Dad, *no*!" Fat tears formed in Bailey's eyes and raced down her cheeks. "Don't listen to her. I don't want you to go! Please, don't."

A thought occurred to him and he swallowed. "Do you wish I were dead, Kayla?"

"No, of course not! I would never wish anyone dead. I'm not a monster. I only want what's best for our daughter."

"Well, we need to come up with a solution, then. Do we need to go to court so I can see my daughter?"

Her mouth hung open. "You would take me before a judge?"

"If that's what I have to do to spend time with my daughter, then yes."

"Unbelievable! So you just think you can show up after *seventeen years* of absence and just decide what's best for everyone else—what's best for our daughter."

"No. I think *she* should decide. She's nearly an

adult. She should be free to choose *whatever* she wants."

"What do you mean by that?"

"She obviously wants me in her life. And I think she should have an opportunity to see what another life looks like."

"What do you mean by *another life*?"

"The *Englisch* world. Maybe she'd like to come live with me in New Jersey for a while."

"No."

He was surprised literal steam wasn't blowing from her ears.

"Absolutely not. And we are not having this conversation. Not without Silas being involved."

Silas. Of course. "Bailey is *our* daughter."

"You *will not* deprive Silas of his rights. He raised her as his own! While you were off doing who-knows-what. And don't you *dare* turn her against him!"

He squeezed his eyes shut. He'd expected to have a pleasant visit with his daughter today, not a boxing match with her mother. "Fine, then. Let's talk with Silas."

"Not now. Another day."

"Fine. When?"

"I'll get in touch and let you know. I'm guessing Bailey already has your phone number?"

"She does." He turned in his seat and lifted a small smile toward his daughter. He wanted to pull the poor thing into an embrace and reassure her that everything would be all right. "May I take you home?"

"I'd like nothing better. But drop us off at the end of the lane. I don't want Silas to see us getting out of your car."

SEVENTEEN

About fifteen minutes later, he pulled into the end of the Millers' driveway. Kayla scrambled out as if the car had been on fire.

Heaviness weighed on his heart as Bailey squeezed through the door's opening from the back seat. He'd never seen her this downtrodden. He pulled his daughter into his arms and held her tight, not caring whether Kayla protested or not. "I love you, Bay. Don't ever forget that," he whispered into her ear. Tears moistened his eyes. If he had to give her up again...

He released his daughter and looked up to see Silas approaching. *Great.* Just great.

"What's going on?" Silas stood next to Kayla, but Josiah was unsure who his question was directed at.

"Apparently, Bailey contacted Josiah, and he came to see her," Kayla said with a sigh.

"But why...what were you doing in his car?" Silas's

gaze ping-ponged from Josiah to Kayla.

"Bailey and I went to IGA and Dairy Queen, where Josiah was apparently waiting for us."

Josiah spoke up now. "I was waiting for *Bailey*. I didn't know Kayla was going to be with her."

Silas turned to Bailey now. "So you contacted Josiah, *and* you've been meeting with him without our permission?" He frowned.

"He's my father." Bailey reached for Josiah's hand, and he squeezed it for support.

"Father or no, you still need to obey. Go to your room, Bailey. We'll discuss your punishment later."

But instead of doing as Silas directed, she stepped closer to Josiah. "No. You're not going to stop me from seeing my dad."

If looks could kill, Josiah would be dead—and probably buried—right now.

Josiah looked down at his daughter. "Bailey, it's okay. I'm not going anywhere," he assured her. "Please. Do as Silas says."

"You're not leaving?" The respect and trust reflecting in her eyes was way more than what he deserved.

"No. I promise." He lifted his eyes in challenge to Silas and Kayla.

"Okay." She nodded, stood on her tiptoes and kissed his cheek, then ran toward the house taking his heart with her. It was completely in her hands. He knew in that moment he'd do anything for her.

Silas glanced back toward the house, probably to be sure Bailey obeyed, then turned to face him. "What do you think you're doing here?"

"My daughter wanted to see me, so I came." He shifted from one foot to the other. "Listen, Silas, I understand why you might be jealous of me."

"Jealous? You think I'm jealous of *you*? You, who got a young innocent girl pregnant out-of-wedlock, then disappeared off the face of the earth and made everyone believe you died?" Silas's crimson face belied his calm stance. "No, jealousy is the farthest thing I feel for you, Josiah."

Yeah, of course. *Perfect* Silas who never did anything wrong. "How did I know you were going to throw that back in my face?"

"If you think you can just sweep in here and steal my wife and my daughter away, you've got another thing coming."

"She's *my* daughter."

"Why do you care all of a sudden? When you left here twelve years ago, you said you didn't want to be tied down with a *fraa* and *kinner*. You wanted another life. Isn't that why you made everyone believe you were dead?"

"If I *didn't* care, do you think I would have come to see my daughter back then? Of course, I cared. I only said those words for *your* benefit, so you wouldn't feel like you stole what should have been mine."

"Stole? I thought you were dead!"

Josiah's eyes shifted to Kayla. "Kayla knew I wasn't."

"Don't pin this on her, Josiah. *She's* not the one who pretended to be dead. You don't know what she went through raising *your dochder* alone."

"You're right, I don't." He turned to Kayla. "I'm sorry. I'm sorry for leaving you in a bind. Like I said before, if I'd known you were pregnant, I probably would have married you and helped you raise our daughter."

"That's not what your letter said." Her arms crossed over her chest.

He pressed his lips together. He'd certainly made a mess of things. "I know. I was still trying to come to grips with things myself when I wrote that. How do you ask a woman, who's in love with your best friend, to leave him for you when you've been absent the last six years of her life? I never claimed to be good with words."

"You should have come to me," Silas said. "I told

you I would have walked away—even though I loved Kayla and Bailey with all my heart, and it would have killed me. I would have."

"I know." Josiah hung his head. "But I had caused so much turmoil. I didn't deserve that privilege. That's why I left the decision up to Kayla. I already knew she'd choose you. You are the better man. Always have been." And there he stood, in all his vulnerability.

"Josiah." Silas sighed. "Let's put this behind us now."

He couldn't help the moisture in his eyes as he shook Silas's outstretched hand, and then when his once-best friend pulled him into an embrace.

"I forgive you. And I hope you'll forgive me too," Silas said.

"I don't know what I need to forgive *you* for."

"For not being the example I should have been. I was angry with you for a long time. It wasn't right."

"Okay, you're forgiven." He nodded. "Thank you, Silas. For everything. I'm proud of the way you raised my daughter. She couldn't have had a better stepfather."

"Do you mean that?"

"Yes, I do."

"That means a lot to hear you say that."

Josiah turned to Kayla. "Will you forgive me now, too?"

She brushed away a tear and nodded.

He wanted to pull her into an embrace, but he restrained himself. "Thank you."

"Why don't you join us for supper?" Silas suggested.

Josiah swallowed down his emotion. He'd get to sit down at a meal at his daughter's table. "Do you mean it?"

Kayla glanced at Silas. "The other children don't even know that Bailey has a different father."

"It looks like it's time we told them."

"Paul's going to have a lot of questions. And your folks." Kayla's brow shot up. She was right.

He needed to set things to rights in Pennsylvania before it was shouted from the rooftops that Josiah Beachy was alive.

"Yeah, maybe supper isn't the best idea just yet." He turned to his friend. "Silas, would you be willing to come to Pennsylvania with me to share the news with my parents?"

"You'd want *me* to come along?"

"I can think of no one better to have at my side," he admitted. "You've always gotten along well with my family."

Silas looked to Kayla. "I need to talk to my *fraa* about it first."

Kayla shook her head. "No. You two go. The sooner everything gets cleared up, the better."

Silas turned to him. "When do you want to go?"

"Is now too soon?"

Silas chuckled. "There's no time like the present. How long will we be gone? I need to let my brother Paul know."

"Probably several days, at least. I'd like to talk to Bailey first, too. I just told her I wasn't leaving." Josiah frowned. And he'd need to call and leave a message for Michael.

"Well, you're not. At least, not permanently, we hope. She'll understand that you have to do this." Silas squeezed his shoulder and smiled now. It was so good to have his friendship back.

EIGHTEEN

Nora sat across the table from Miriam, a warm mug between her hands. "Well, I'm glad Josiah's making things right with his family."

"*Jah*, that's *gut*." Miriam smiled. "You know what this means, don't you?"

"What does it mean?" Was she missing something?

"It means that he intends on letting everyone know he's still alive because he wants to be part of Bailey's life. I bet he'll become Plain again. And when he does, he'll need a *fraa*."

Nora practically snorted with laughter. "I think you're jumping to conclusions. The last thing I got from Josiah is that he had no intentions of becoming Amish again."

"But you said he kissed you."

Nora squeezed her eyes close. *Boy, did he ever.* "I'm trying to forget that. It's easier that way." Otherwise, she'd dwell on it way too much. "He only wants friendship."

"Then why did he kiss you?" Miriam had a point.

"He just got carried away in the moment. We both did." She frowned. "Miriam, I have the girls to think about. It wouldn't be good to let them make attachments to Josiah if he's going to leave someday soon."

"I don't think he's going to leave his *dochder*."

"Yeah, but he works in New Jersey. How is he going to make that work?"

"I don't know the answer to that." She shrugged. "But he brought his computer. He's been working here, although he constantly needs to recharge his battery. It's a *gut* thing Sammy has a generator. Josiah said he could charge it in the car but it takes a lot more juice."

"Juice?" Her nose scrunched up. "What does juice have to do with it?"

Miriam laughed and lifted a shoulder. "I don't know. I think that might be another word for electric?"

"It's silly."

"I didn't make it up. Maybe Josiah did. I'll have to ask Michael if he heard of it before. But my point is, he *can* work from here. It's what he's been doing between helping out on the farm and spending time with Bailey. And you." Her grin widened.

"Still. It's an *Englisch* job. The leaders would never approve of it."

"Would you ever consider becoming an *Englischer* then?"

"Absolutely not. And you shouldn't be suggesting it. What would I do without the support of our people? You know that at least half of the *Englisch* marriages fail."

"I know. It's sad. I can kind of see why, though. It seems like *Englisch* families are always so busy. They don't spend enough time together. I don't even know if they share one meal together, let alone every meal."

"I missed that with Andy. He was gone so much. I was lonely a lot." Nora frowned. "I couldn't even imagine being *Englisch*."

"And I don't want you to be."

"The Plain life is something I'm not willing to give up. Not even for the love of a husband."

Bailey stared up at the clock, wondering where her dads were at right now. She'd been praying for them since the moment they left. Had they made it to Pennsylvania yet? She wished she could be there to see

Grossdawdi and *Grossmammi* Beachy's reaction to her father being alive.

Her heart filled with gladness as she thought of her father reconciling with her mother and stepfather. And it appeared Dad and Silas were becoming friends again, something they hadn't been since they were still in their teens. She'd pray that his reunion with his folks would go well too.

Life had never been so exciting and she couldn't wait to see what the future held. Since her father stepped back into her life, she'd thought of little else. Hopefully, they'd always have a *gut* relationship. *Ach*, she just loved him to pieces!

The bell jingled, pulling her from her thoughts. Her smile grew wide as she spotted her best friend— "aunt" Emily, who was only a year older than she was. "Emily! *Ach*, it feels like it's been forever!"

"Where have you been hiding? You didn't come to the last singing." Emily engulfed her in a hug.

"I know. I've been busy." She giggled. "If I tell you a secret, do you promise not to tell anyone—well, at least for a while?"

Emily smiled. "You know I'm a *gut* secret keeper."

"You can't tell anyone, not till I say, 'cause it's gonna be a big surprise."

"What is it already?"

"Okay." She was so giddy she could hardly stand it. "My dad..." She took a deep breath.

"Silas, my big *bruder*." She nodded.

"*Nee*. My *real* dad, Josiah Beachy."

"What about him?"

"I found out that he's alive."

Emily gasped and covered her mouth.

"I know. Anyway. He came here to see me. And I met him."

Emily's eyes grew wide. "You're pulling my leg."

She shook her head adamantly. "I'm not. I'm telling the truth. Honest."

"Your *dat* is alive?"

"He really is. He's so handsome, Emily!" She bounced on her toes. "He took me for ice cream and we talked a long time. I love him so much."

"But how can he be alive?"

"I don't know. He just is. You promised not to tell. You can't tell *anyone*."

"I won't. I said I wouldn't." She squealed. "When do I get to meet him?"

"I don't know. He and Silas went to Pennsylvania to—"

"Pennsylvania?"

"*Ach*, if you'd quit interrupting, I can finish. Yes, Pennsylvania. That's where Josiah's folks live. You met them when they came here before, *Grossdawdi* and *Grossmammi* Beachy."

She nodded. "I remember."

"Anyway, they're gonna find out that my dad is alive, so I've been praying for them. You know, that *Dawdi* Alvin doesn't get a heart attack or that *Mammi* Ada doesn't faint. Because *Mamm* said that they might."

Emily giggled.

"It's not funny." Bailey jammed a hand on her hip. "It could really happen!"

"I know. I'm sorry."

The bell jingled again and Emily's sister walked in. "What's taking you so long, Emily? It's hot out in that buggy. There's hardly any breeze today."

"I'm coming, Martha! I'll be out in a little bit. I'm not done talking to Bailey."

"Well, hurry up!" She stomped her foot.

"We're not gonna talk with you here."

"Why not? It's not like you two have anything important to say."

"How do you know?"

"Because I do."

"*Geh*, Martha! You're such an *alt maedel*."

"I am not!"

"Uh huh, you're twenty-seven. That makes you an

alt maedel." Emily turned to Bailey. "It's because she's a gossip and everyone knows it."

Bailey covered her mouth. *Oh my.*

Martha stormed out of the store.

Emily giggled. "I knew that would make her leave."

"You shouldn't say that to your *schweschder.*" Bailey felt bad for her aunt Martha. *Sometimes.*

"She teases me all the time."

"Still. You should be kind."

"Bailey, I have to tell you something." Emily turned serious. "You're not going to like it."

Bailey frowned. "What?"

"It's about Timothy. He was at the singing on Sunday, you know."

"*Jah.*"

"Well, he took MaryAnn Kinsinger home."

"He said his folks would probably make him take someone home to prove we weren't—"

"No, Bailey. He likes her. And people have been saying that you were with an *Englischer.*"

"It was my dad." But, of course, she couldn't tell anyone that.

"They said you were in a fancy car, and people saw you hugging him. Timothy was really mad."

"What? Why didn't he come and talk to me if he thought I was seeing an *Englisch* guy?"

Emily shrugged. "I don't know."

"Who saw me? Who is spreading these lies?"

"I don't know. That's just the word that's been going around. Everyone thinks you're going to jump the fence."

"I am *not* going to jump the fence!" Tears filled her eyes.

"I know that you would never." Emily squeezed her hand. "I told you that you wouldn't like it. But you needed to know."

"How can Timothy do that to me?" She cried. "He said he was going to wait!"

Emily shrugged. "I'm sorry. I hated to tell you. I knew you would cry." Tears pricked Emily's own eyes and she brushed them away with her sleeve. "Anyway, I gotta go. Martha's probably having a fit by now."

Emily stepped near and hugged Bailey. "I'll pray for you. And for your *dat*."

"*Denki*, Emily." She sniffled.

As soon as her friend stepped out the door, Bailey broke down and sobbed.

NINETEEN

Josiah's eyes misted as he drove up to his folks' farmhouse—a place he hadn't seen in a long, long time. It had hardly changed in the eighteen years he'd been gone. The white two-story house was decorated exactly the same. Blue curtains in the windows, several colorful hanging flower pots adorned the wraparound porch. Even the same wooden chairs invited him to come, sit down, and enjoy a refreshing glass of *Mamm's* peppermint iced tea.

He'd called his brother Jaden to let him know he was coming. Jaden being there, along with Silas, would give him the boost of confidence and moral support he knew would be needed. But this...this was going to be the most difficult thing he'd done in his entire life. At least his folks already knew about Bailey.

He killed the engine and glanced at his friend.

"This is hard, Silas. I don't know if I can do it."

Silas reached over and squeezed his shoulder. "With God, you can. Let's pray for *Der Herr* to give you the strength you need."

"Yeah, okay." He blew out a breath.

They both bowed their heads. Josiah's head popped up in surprise when Silas began praying aloud.

"Dear God, I come to You on behalf of my friend, Josiah Beachy. You know that he has done much wrong and has hurt a lot of people. Today, we ask that You bring healing. Today, we ask that You give Josiah the strength that he needs to share the truth with his family. Today, we ask that You change his life for the better. Make him a new man and give him a new start. We ask this in Jesus' name. Amen."

"Thank you."

"Let's do this." Silas looked at him "You ready?"

He nodded and blew out a breath.

It was evening, so his folks were likely enjoying supper at the moment. He and Silas approached the porch, his legs feeling more sluggish with every step. *In a few moments, the most awkward part will be over with,* he told himself. He knocked on the door—something he'd never done before.

To his relief, Jaden answered. "They're at the

supper table," Jaden whispered.

"What should we...should we just walk in there?"

"*Nee*, I'll call them over." Jaden walked into the other room. "*Mamm, Dat,* there's someone here to see you."

"Invite them in," his father said.

Jaden walked to where they could see him. "You heard him. *Kumm.*"

Josiah flicked a worried look at Silas, who nudged him forward.

"Just get it over with," Silas whispered.

One foot in front of the other, Josiah moved toward the kitchen. Jaden put up a hand to halt him before their parents saw him.

"*Mamm, Dat,*" Jaden began. "There is someone here. It's going to be a really big surprise and I think I need to warn you, first."

"What are you talking about, *sohn*?" His father's chair scraped the floor. He was getting up.

Josiah and Silas stepped into the dining area. "*Mamm, Dat,* it's me, Josiah. I'm alive."

His mother squealed. Like a flash of lightning, she had vacated her seat and wrapped him in a motherly embrace. "I knew it! I knew it all along. In my heart of hearts, I knew. I never could believe that you were dead. I never accepted it."

He awkwardly patted his mother's back. He never remembered her being this affectionate.

She stepped back and examined him. "Yep, it's definitely our Josiah. *Kumm*, Alvin." She waved his father over with her hand.

His father eyed him suspiciously. "Where have you been the last eighteen years?"

He shrugged. "Just drifting around, I guess."

"Drifting around?" He frowned.

"I've been working in New Jersey for the last ten years. Before that, I was traveling abroad and I was in school."

"So, you let your family believe you were dead so you could go off and see the world?"

He didn't blame his father for being upset.

"It was wrong. I'm sorry, *Dat*, *Mamm*. I've come asking for forgiveness."

Mamm put a hand on *Dat's* arm. "Our *sohn* is home now. Let us rejoice," she pleaded.

His father glanced from him to his mom, to Silas to Jaden, then nodded. "*Jah*, okay. *Kumm*, sit. Have some supper."

Josiah released a long breath. He looked at Silas, who nodded and smiled.

"I don't know about you, but I'm starving," Silas said.

His mother set two more plates at the table. "There is plenty. Your other brothers are gone for a few days."

Josiah frowned. He'd hoped he'd get to reconcile with the whole family. But he supposed his folks were enough for now.

His father looked at Josiah and a faint smile teased his lips. His father reached for his hand. "Let us pray and thank *Der Herr*. For the prodigal has come home."

Josiah bowed his head. It felt like a ten-pound weight had been lifted from his shoulders. He uttered his own silent prayer of thanksgiving.

The remainder of the evening was mostly joyous as they all caught up on each other's lives. Silas and Jaden admitted their part in the keeping of Josiah's secret, but Josiah accepted full blame for it. His folks had been thrilled to hear that he'd connected with Bailey.

"Are you planning to settle and join the *g'may* now?" His father's voice sounded hopeful.

"I haven't decided exactly what I'm going to do just yet. But because Bailey's in Indiana, I might just end up moving out that way too."

"And I hear he's got an eye on a certain Amish widow as well." Silas smiled.

"Wait." Josiah stared at him. "How did you know that? Where did you—Michael! You heard it from Michael, didn't you?"

His parents looked back and forth at each other as if they harbored some secret. They were obviously pleased with his words, although he'd said nothing about joining the Amish church.

Josiah beheld the rural farm scenery as fireflies sprouted from the grass, taking their evening flight, and lighting up the night. He sipped on a refreshing glass of *Mamm's* peppermint iced tea. Tonight, he'd be tucked away in a bed he hadn't occupied in eighteen years with his *Mammi's* quilt covering him in a work of love. And all the world—or at least *his* world—was right once again.

TWENTY

Bailey had been a mess ever since Emily had shared the news about Timothy with her. She probably shouldn't be working in the store in such a state, but *Mamm* had been busy in the house with the *kinner* and the chores, especially since Silas had been gone. Technically, Bailey had the easy job.

Just so long as Timothy or MaryAnn Kinsinger didn't come in. And just the thought of Timothy's betrayal caused her to break down in tears—again.

She hardly believed it until she saw them looking at each other at meeting on Sunday, and then the singing. She should have never attended the singing, but she'd hoped to get a chance to talk to Timothy in private. It never happened. And then, at the end, sure enough, he'd taken MaryAnn Kinsinger home. What had she been thinking?

She didn't think her heart could stand to go to

another singing ever again. She couldn't even imagine riding home with anyone except Timothy.

"Bailey!" *Onkel* Paul rushed into the store, his eyes frantic. "Is your *mamm* here?"

"*Nee*, she's at the house with the *kinner*. Why?"

"It's Jenny. The *boppli's* coming!"

"*Ach*, for real?"

"*Jah*. Could you close up the store and go watch the *kinner* for your *mamm*? I'm going to tell her about Jenny so she can go stay with her, then I'm going to fetch the midwife."

"Why don't you call her on the phone?"

"Tried. No answer. But I have an idea where she might be. Anyway, I need to hurry." He charged out of the store.

"Uh, *jah*. Okay. Go!" Excitement charged through Bailey's veins at the thought of holding another tiny niece or nephew in her arms. This would be their fifth child.

Someday, *Gott* willing and at the right time, Bailey hoped to have a *boppli* of her own. Sorrow clenched her heart when she realized it would likely never be with Timothy—the only one she'd imagined as the father of her *kinner*.

Josiah couldn't wipe the smile off his face as he and Silas traveled back to Indiana. The meeting with his folks had gone better than he could imagine. Thankfully, for him, forgiveness was the Amish way and a virtue held dear by their culture. To not forgive would be to pass judgement on someone, and that right belonged to God alone. Which made Him wonder...

"I want to ask you something, Silas."

"About what?"

"It was something that Bailey said. And something that I've observed with you and Michael and Sammy."

"What's that?"

"Well, God. Bailey mentioned having Jesus in your heart. I'd never heard that preached in the Amish church. Is that really a thing?"

He nodded. "I never knew that it was before studying it. And technically, the phrase 'Jesus in your heart' is not in the Bible, but the concept is. *Ach*, if I had my Bible here, I could show you." He frowned.

Josiah pulled his phone out of his pocket. "Here, you can look it up on this."

Silas held the phone in his hand and stared down at it.

"See that little microphone in the rectangular box right there. Tap it with your finger then speak what you want it to find."

Silas did as told. "Okay, here is one place that talks about it. It's in Ephesians, so it was written by the Apostle Paul. He writes here, *That he would grant you, according to the riches of his glory, to be strengthened with might by his Spirit in the inner man; That Christ may dwell in your hearts by faith; that ye, being rooted and grounded in love, May be able to comprehend with all saints what is the breadth, and length, and depth, and height; And to know the love of Christ, which passeth knowledge, that ye might be filled with all the fullness of God.*"

Josiah's lips twisted. "You understand all that?"

Silas shrugged. "I think so. But what I wanted you to see is that this passage mentions the concept three times. It talks about God's Spirit being *in* the inner man, Christ dwelling *in* your heart by faith, and being *filled* with all the fullness of God. Now, he's *only* talking to believers. God does not dwell in everyone's heart, only those who have trusted in Christ."

Josiah nodded. "I think I'm getting it. Maybe." He chuckled.

"You're not getting it." Silas frowned. "Let me explain it this way. When a person accepts Jesus as their Saviour—"

"Wait. What do you mean by that...*accepts* Jesus?"

"Okay. The Bible says that *all have sinned.* It also

says that *the wages of sin is death*. Do you understand that much?"

"Well, I *definitely* know that I have sinned. But wages?"

"What our sin earns us—death."

"Okay."

"We sin because we are born in the likeness of Adam."

"But I thought we were born in the likeness of God?"

"No. Adam was originally. When he sinned, he lost that. He died *spiritually*. That's why God told him that if he ate of the fruit from the tree of the knowledge of good and evil, that he would surely die. And I don't know if I'll ever figure out why they ate that fruit. They already knew good. Why would they *want* to know evil?"

Josiah shrugged. "Curiosity, maybe?"

"I guess curiosity kills more than the cat." Silas shook his head. "Anyway, Adam's sin is handed down to each person born, so we are all sinners. And because of his sin, the first death occurred."

"Are you referring to Cain and Abel?"

"Yes and no. That was the first *murder*. The first *physical* death was when God had to cover Adam and Eve with coats of skins. They tried to cover themselves with leaves but it wasn't good enough. And that was a picture, an example, for what is required of us."

"What do you mean?"

"Well, payment for sin requires a blood sacrifice. We cannot pay for it with our own deeds, our own works, because it is not what is required. *Without the shedding of blood, there is no remission.* But when Jesus died on the cross and shed His perfect sinless blood, he became the sacrifice for all men, for all time. He died once, for all. So, when we accept Jesus' sacrifice as a payment for our sin, it is acceptable to God. His blood justifies us before God."

It was beginning to make sense. Josiah smiled. "Okay, I get that part. Jesus paid for sin."

"Right. The Bible says *that if thou shalt confess with thy mouth the Lord Jesus, and shalt believe in thine heart that God hath raised him from the dead, thou shalt be saved. For with the heart man believeth unto righteousness; and with the mouth confession is made unto salvation.*" Silas studied him. "So, Jesus is called the second Adam. In the first Adam, all die. So, in the same way, through the second Adam—in Christ—all can be made alive. And the life that Jesus gives is everlasting life. Remember I said how *the wages of sin is death*?"

"Yeah."

"Well, the second part of that verse is *but the gift of God is eternal life through Jesus Christ our Lord.*"

"So, eternal life is a gift?"

"Yes. Which means you cannot earn it. The only way for you to get the gift is by receiving it. Calling upon the Lord for salvation. *For whosoever shall call upon the name of the Lord shall be saved.*"

"You're telling me that all a person needs to do to get eternal life is to believe and ask God? That sounds so simple." Was it really?

"Exactly. God made it simple because He wants everyone to be saved. It cost Him His Son. Not one drop of His blood need be wasted. But unfortunately, not all choose God's way. Many choose their own way. And sadly, God's Word says that their own way leads to death and hell."

"I want to choose God's way. Does that mean I have to be Amish, though?"

"Did you see the word 'Amish' in any of the verses I just quoted?"

He frowned. "No."

"It's not even in the Bible."

"It isn't? But I thought..." He shrugged. "I don't know what I thought. Except that some Amish leaders say that you go to hell if you leave the Amish church. I'm confused."

"Do you remember the story of when God led the Israelites out of Egypt?"

"Yeah."

"Well, remember the plague about the death of the first born?"

He nodded.

"The Israelites were told to kill a lamb and put the blood on the doorposts. Do you remember what He said?"

"No."

"God said, "When I see the blood, I will pass over you." He didn't say, "when I see that you're an Israelite or in our case Amish, or Catholic or Baptist or Mormon or whatever. He didn't say when I see all the good works you've done." It was the blood. And only the blood. The blood of Christ is what cleanses us and saves us, if we believe."

"Wow."

"That's why it's important to read your Bible. When you hear something that is different than what the Bible says, always stick with the Bible. God is right one hundred percent of the time. Man, whether Amish or not, is often wrong or has a wrong understanding. That is why the Bible urges us to study the Scriptures. Know what God says. Learn to rightly divide God's Word. If you study and pray and seek

God, He will give you wisdom and discernment."

"Wow, I feel like you have so much more of that than I do." Josiah shook his head.

"Only because I've done what I just told you. I read and I study and I pray. And sometimes, if there is something I don't understand or can't figure out or it seems to contradict, I'll ask someone who has more spiritual wisdom than I do."

"Who? Your bishop?"

"I do occasionally talk to Bishop Bontrager about the Bible. But the person that led me to the Lord and opened my eyes to God's Word was a Christian pastor. He was just a driver for me at first. And then we started talking. I was amazed at how many answers he had, answers to questions the bishop didn't know. And he found them in the Bible. I didn't even know that they were there."

"Can I...would you want to study with me?"

"I'd love that. You know, Sammy—Michael's *grossdawdi*, is very wise when it comes to the Bible. You should sit down and talk to him sometime."

"Okay. I think I will." He glanced at his friend. "I want to be saved. But I don't know how to do it— how to seal the deal, so to speak."

Silas smiled. "That's wonderful. Do you want me to pray with you?"

"Would you, please? Out loud, like last time?"

"Sure. But you've got to keep your eyes open to drive." Silas chuckled.

"Will do."

Silas bowed his head. "Dear God, first of all, I want to thank You for my friend, Josiah. I'm so happy that he wants to be saved. Thank You for touching his heart. Please give him wisdom and understanding in the days to come." Silas lifted his head and looked at Josiah. "Do you want to pray now?"

He grimaced. "I'm not sure how, or what to say."

"Do you want me to help you?"

"Please?"

"Well, there are no special words, they just need to be sincere and from *your* heart. So, if you believe what I am about to say, then repeat the words."

Josiah nodded. "Sounds good."

"Dear God, I know that I am a sinner and that sin leads to death and hell."

Josiah repeated the words.

"I believe with my heart that Jesus Christ died and shed His blood for me to wash away my sins."

He agreed aloud.

"And I believe that He was buried, and rose from the dead, and is now alive."

Josiah repeated.

"Please save me, and come into my heart and life, and make me a new man."

He again reiterated Silas's words.

"Thank You for Your gift of eternal life that You have placed within me. Please help me to live for You. Amen."

Josiah repeated the last words, then smiled broadly. "I'm saved now." Just saying the words made his heart burst with joy. He was saved now!

"If you were sincere, then yes, you *are* saved now." Silas grinned. "You are now on your way to Heaven. You no longer need to fear hell. God is and will forever be with you, inside you, every second of every day. The gift that God gives, no man can take away. The devil may try to convince you otherwise, but you have the promises of God's Word."

"And God is right one hundred percent of the time."

"Well done, my friend!" Silas high-fived him.

"I can't wait to go home and share the news with Bailey!" He smiled so much, his cheeks ached.

"Home?"

"Well, temporary, at least."

"Why don't you pray and see what God would have you do?" Silas's brow arched.

"That's a great idea, my friend."

TWENTY-ONE

Silas twisted toward Josiah as they turned onto the home stretch. "So, you and Michael are going to take over for the day while Miriam and Nora have a free day to themselves?"

"Yeah, but I want to have some stuff for them to do. Michael and I have a couple of ideas."

"Like what?" Silas grinned.

"I'm thinking they would really enjoy a Swedish massage at a spa. Michael suggested a movie if we can find any good ones playing. Maybe a nice lunch somewhere, and some money to go girl shopping."

"Oh, they're going to love that." Silas frowned. "Do you think my *fraa* can get in on that?"

"Kayla? I don't see why not. As long as you pay for her part." He chuckled. "That's a lot of kids."

"I'd suggest Paul's *fraa* too, but she's about to have a *boppli* any day now." He clapped his hands together.

"And we can enlist my sisters, Emily and Martha, to help Bailey. And we'll be there too, of course."

"And we can all grill out in the evening when they return home."

"Sounds good to me. Whose place are we going to have it at?"

"Michael probably wouldn't mind, but I think your place is bigger."

"The house is, but Sammy has more yard for the *kinner* to play in."

"You have a point. Well, we can talk to Michael and Sammy and see what they say."

Josiah turned into Silas's driveway.

"Hmm...that's strange. It looks like the store's closed. It's usually open today." Silas frowned. "Will you stop and let me out?"

Josiah stopped just past the store but waited for Silas to return before continuing on.

Silas hopped back in. "I could have walked."

"I know. What's up?"

"I don't know. It's closed. I hope everything's okay."

Josiah parked the vehicle in front of Silas's home.

"I'll go see what's up with Kayla. Did you want to see Bailey?"

"Of course." Josiah smiled. He had to tell her all about his good news.

They walked into the house together. Little ones were crying and there were toys and clothes throughout the living room.

A worried look flashed across Silas's face. "Uh, Kayla?" he called out.

"*Ach*, you need to stop crying!" It was Bailey's voice echoing down the hall.

"Kayla? Bailey? What's going on?"

A half-dressed little one bolted down the hallway toward Silas, Bailey was on his heels. "Oh, no you don't!" She glanced up and saw them, then sighed in relief. "Oh good! You're finally home," she moaned.

"What's going on? Where's *Mamm*?" Silas frowned.

"*Ach*, *Aenti* Jenny is having her *boppli* right now. I'm stuck with diaper duty for these little rascals." She wiped sweat from her forehead. "Remind me never to have a thousand children."

Josiah chuckled.

"You only got seven under your charge," Silas said, as if it were no big deal. "Where are Judah and Shiloh? Aren't they helping?"

"Shiloh went with *Mamm*. Lucky. And I think Judah said he was going fishing. Besides, he'd probably be more trouble than he's worth. Before he left, he gave Lucas his markers to use. Who gives a two-year-old markers? He marked up all the wall in his and Daniel's room. I sent him straight to bed, but I doubt he's still napping. I'm afraid to see what mischief he's up to next."

Silas and Josiah eyed each other, both suppressing a grin.

"I better check," Silas volunteered. "Where are the others?"

"Sierra is supposed to be keeping Daniel and Lydia occupied at the table." She grabbed the little one by the dress. Josiah wasn't sure whether it was a girl or a boy. "Oh, no! Will you take Aaron, *Dat,* and put his diaper on? He just soiled his dress again!"

She shook a finger at the little one, who giggled in return. "I just put that on you. You little stinker." She tickled his tummy.

"*Ach.*" Silas shook his head. "*Jah*, I'll take him. Unless, your other *dat* would like to take a turn."

Josiah held up his hands. "No, thank you. He's all yours."

Bailey turned to Josiah. "I don't know how *Mamm* does it."

"It looks like she has a good helper or two." Josiah smiled, attempting to encourage his daughter.

She rolled her eyes. "Sometimes, I feel like I just want to get away."

"I know what you mean."

"Not that I want to leave and become *Englisch* or anything like that. Just a little vacation or something."

Silas returned with two little ones in tow. "How about if your *Englisch dat* and I watch the little ones while you and Sierra fix supper?"

"I have a better idea. Let's order pizza," Josiah suggested.

"Pizza!" The children all clapped their hands.

"No turning back now." Silas chuckled.

Josiah eyed his friend. "And I'm buying."

"I won't argue with that." Silas grinned. He turned to Bailey. "Your *dat* has something to tell you."

"That's right." Josiah's smile widened and he studied Bailey. "I have Jesus in my heart now!"

Bailey squealed and threw her arms around him. "For real?"

"For real." He chuckled. "That was the reaction I was hoping for."

Hours later, as Josiah settled in for the night in Michael's spare bedroom, he mulled over Bailey's words. He'd been pondering quite a few things lately. His job in New Jersey. Nora. His parents. Returning to the Plain community. Bailey. His future. Their future. His new-found relationship with Christ.

Silas was right. He needed to pray.

TWENTY-TWO

Nora, Miriam, and Kayla stepped out of the vehicle in front of the shopping center. Today had proven to be exciting so far. But Nora admitted to herself that she felt a little awkward around Kayla now. Did Kayla know that there was anything between Nora and Josiah? *Was* there anything going on between Nora and Josiah? She wasn't even sure herself.

Nora glanced at Kayla, thinking about her past relationship with Josiah and the daughter they'd created together. Kayla was a beautiful woman. It was easy to see how Josiah would have been attracted to her, especially if he'd met her when they were younger, and at the beach. Nora had only been to the beach once, but she'd seen the types of clothing *Englischers* wore when sunbathing. She could see how a young man would have trouble keeping his eyes focused on *Der Herr* with temptation all around.

But you shouldn't judge, she chided herself.

"Okay," Miriam said. "Michael said to open up number one when we were dropped off here." She handed an envelope to each of them marked with a one.

They looked at each other and smiled, then opened their envelopes. Each one contained a note and money. Nora opened the note, which she figured was in Josiah's handwriting.

> Nora,
>   A woman like you is hard to resist. Have fun shopping, but save me a kiss.
>   JB

She gasped at the words.

"What?" Miriam scrunched near. "What did he write?"

Nora quickly hid her note. "I don't think anyone else is supposed to read this." She knew her cheeks must be red as raspberries. "What does yours say?"

"Uh...this is definitely for my eyes only!" Miriam giggled.

"*Jah*, mine too." Kayla said.

"Well, then." Miriam linked her arms with both

ladies. "We'll just have to be called the secret keepers. Shall we go shopping now?"

An hour and a half later, their *Englisch* driver pulled up. "Time for our next adventure!" Miriam squealed.

Nora had to admit this was exciting.

Miriam handed both Kayla and Nora their second envelope when they reached their next destination. The driver promised to be back in an hour. A smile played on her lips as she pulled out the next note.

> Nora,
>   Shopping is tiring and you need a rest, enjoy a massage and you'll feel your best. When you return home, you won't know what to do, do I deserve one kiss or will I get two? ☺
>   J.B.

Nora giggled and clasped her hand over her mouth. "Oh, my."

"What secrets are you hiding?" Miriam snickered, bumping her hip into Nora's.

"Wouldn't you like to know?" She teased.

"And you thought Josiah wasn't interested." Miriam laughed. "I'm thinking he's changing your mind?"

Kayla gasped. "Josiah?" She eyed Nora and Miriam.

"Beachy?"

"*Jah*," Miriam confirmed.

"I'm sorry," Nora said. "Maybe I should have asked you if you minded. But I didn't even know at first."

Kayla's hand swatted the air in front of her. "No need to ask me. I'm a very happily married woman. Josiah is free to date whomever he chooses without my permission."

"I know, it's just..." She shrugged.

To her surprise, Kayla draped an arm around her shoulder. "I'm just glad that he found a good woman."

Nora's eyes misted. "*Denki.* That means a lot."

"If you and Josiah married, you'd be Bailey's stepmom." Kayla smiled.

"She's a really sweet girl."

Kayla nodded. "She really is. But she can be a firecracker."

"Josiah loves her so much. He lights up every time he talks about her."

"I'm glad to hear that. I hope they can have a good, positive relationship."

"It seems like they do."

"Well, ladies." Miriam sighed dramatically. "Let's go relax."

The remainder of their special day was just as

enjoyable. The women shared a delicious lunch, a carriage ride down by the river—which they all thought was a little silly since they drove horses and buggies all the time—but it was fun nonetheless, and then a frivolous but sweet movie.

Nora cherished every note from Josiah, as each one built on the last. But goodness, when would she be able to give him all those kisses? Her skin tingled just thinking about being close to him, breathing in his faint masculine scent—cologne or body wash or whatever it was, his mouth on hers.

Anticipation filled her as their driver pulled into the lane at Sammy Eicher's place. Their entire group of friends was there, including Silas's two younger sisters, who'd assisted Bailey and the men with babysitting all the *kinner*. Or keeping them all alive and safe was probably more like it. Silas's brother Paul, and his *fraa*, Jenny, had arrived at the same time their vehicle had pulled up. She couldn't wait to see the tiny *boppli* Jenny had given birth to a little over a week ago.

Nora carried her small bag of purchases, along with her purse, concealing Josiah's promises of romance. If she had believed he *might* be interested in her prior to this outing, his notes left no doubt. Her gaze scanned the play area until she spotted her daughters. Sylvia was on one of the swings attempting to pump her legs, while Josiah lightly pushed her and another little boy from behind. Esther sat at a picnic table with several of the other *kinner* and it looked like they were working on a craft project. A relieved breath escaped her lips. She'd hardly been away from her precious daughters since they'd been born. Just seeing them triggered a smile.

The moment she was about to turn away to drop her things off inside, Josiah strode in her direction. Mischief sparkled in his eyes. *Ach*, he didn't intend to claim his kisses here in public, did he? Her heartbeat quickened with each step closer to her he came.

He stopped a couple of feet away from her, to her relief. "Did you have a good time?"

"*Ach*, it was *wunderbaar*! *Denki*."

He took a step closer and lowered his voice. "Oh, you can thank me later."

Her pulse raced at his nearness. She lifted the items she held. "I should...uh...maybe put these inside somewhere."

"Okay, do you mind if I join you?"

She shook her head.

"I hope you ladies still have an appetite because the sausages and burgers will be ready in just a little bit." He followed her up the front porch, where Jenny and

Paul sat on the porch swing with their new *boppli*, then into the house. She placed her purse and her bag into a nook in the china hutch. When she spun around, she hadn't expected Josiah to be so close. But he hadn't attempted to claim any kisses.

"I...uh...need to talk to you about something." His voice was serious. "May I drive you and the girls home tonight?"

"That's probably a good idea since my buggy isn't here. We would appreciate that."

"About the notes. If that makes you uncomfortable...I didn't intend to force anything."

"I have something for you, actually." She smiled to herself. "Okay, close your eyes." As quietly as possible, she reached into her bag.

A smile of anticipation danced on his lips.

She leaned close and whispered in his ear, "Are you ready?"

His voice turned husky. "Oh, I'm ready. How long do I have to wait? You're killing me."

She reached for his hand and lightly massaged it with her fingers before placing a chocolate Hershey's Kiss in his palm.

His eyes popped open and he looked down at his hand. "Hey, that's cheating." He chuckled.

She reached her hand up to caress his cheek, gazing

into his eyes. "You'll get your second kiss tonight when you drop me off."

Then she turned and headed outside.

◦⌒⌒◦

"Hey, Josiah, would you mind taking her off my hands?" Paul asked, holding his tiny *boppli*. "I just got challenged to a game of corn hole and I plan to beat the pants off my *bruder*."

"Uh, sure." Josiah shrugged.

"You have to keep a hand under her head." Paul handed over the bundle of blankets. Wasn't the little one hot under all that? What would he know? He had zero experience with tiny babies.

"I can do that." The little thing weighed absolutely nothing.

"We'll see who beats who," Silas called back.

"All talk and no action," Paul tossed his first bean bag into the hole. "See? That's how it's done." He turned to his wife and flexed his bicep. "Ladies."

"Oh, brother." Silas laughed. "Did you forget that I beat you last time?"

"You cheated."

"How do you cheat at corn hole?"

The baby squirmed in his arms, yanking Josiah's attention away from the game. Her little hand had wrapped its way around his finger. She puckered her rose petal lips and whimpered. Her tiny chest rose and fell quickly for a second or two, then she snuggled back into a place of comfort. Her mouth began making a sucking motion while she slept. It was the most adorable thing he'd ever seen. His heart instantly melted. *Ach*, he wanted one of his own!

His eyes shot to Nora, who stood with the other women. But instead of watching the game or the *kinner* or her female companions, her gaze had been fixed on him. A look of pleasure graced her countenance.

Was she thinking the same thing he was? He hoped so.

TWENTY-THREE

*B*ailey needed to sit down and have a talk with her folks, but she feared they might not be happy with what she had to say. She still needed to say it, though.

After the *kinner* had been put down to bed for the evening, she joined them in the living room. "I wanted to talk to y'all about something."

"Say on," Silas urged.

"Well, it's about..." Tears surfaced in her eyes. *Ach,* she was never going to get through this if she was crying already. She forced them away. "It's about Timothy. He's seeing another girl." Her voice cracked.

Mamm was at her side in a split second and Silas reached over and touched her knee.

"Oh, I'm sorry, sweetie," *Mamm* said, rubbing her back.

"The thing is," she forged on, "I don't want to stay here and watch them. I don't want to go to any more singings. And I don't want to see them glancing at each other during church." She brushed away more tears.

Silas frowned. He was obviously out of his comfort zone with this subject.

"Do you think...would it be possible if I went and stayed with my dad for a while?"

Mamm and Silas looked at each other. It was that silent communication that she'd seen many married couples do.

She continued. "He said he was going to go back to New Jersey to pack up his stuff and get things in order. I'd like to go with him. He already said he'd love it if I came along. And he said we could visit with *Mammi* and *Dawdi* Beachy for a few days, if we wanted to. I haven't seen them in a long time."

She looked from Silas to her mother. Silas gave *Mamm* a nod that was ever so slight, she may have missed it if she hadn't been paying close attention.

"Let us discuss it for a minute," *Mamm* said.

Bailey waited patiently on the couch, while she heard muffled voices coming from her folks' bedroom. She wondered what exactly they were discussing.

A few moments later, they emerged from their room. Silas spoke, "Your mother and I have agreed to let you do this."

She felt like squealing.

"However," he continued, "we are a little worried about your dad's *Englisch* influence on you."

"But he's going to become Amish," she reasoned.

"Did he tell you this?"

"No. But I'm pretty sure and certain he's going to marry Nora Schwartz."

"Did he say that?" Silas glanced at *Mamm*.

"No, but did you see the way they look at each other?"

"Bailey," Silas held up his hand. "That's not...*ach*."

"That's gossip, Bailey," *Mamm* warned. She never liked it when Bailey speculated about things.

"I'm not telling anyone but you. Just wait. You'll see that I'm right." She eyed them. "Why else would he be going to New Jersey to pick up his stuff and come back here?"

"He wants to be near *you*, baby," *Mamm* said.

"Well, you don't need to worry about me. I have no intentions of becoming an *Englischer*. Their lives are way too complicated."

Silas studied her. "Just be on your guard."

"I'm so excited that we're going to be together that

long. I can teach him more about Jesus."

Silas smiled now. "I'm sure he'd like that."

"Silas." Bailey frowned. "I don't want you to think that you're not important to me anymore or that I don't love you." She stood up, then leaned down to hug him. "*Denki* for all you've done for me. I couldn't have asked for a better stepfather."

He rose to meet her and she felt his embrace tighten around her, then he released her. When she pulled back, she was sure and certain she noticed moisture shimmering in his eyes.

Josiah sat across from Nora at her kitchen table. He really liked her home. The ambiance was calm and relaxing. It was almost like a cabin in the woods, with a large meadow out back, which was sort of what it was. He could imagine living here.

He reached for her hands. "How do you feel about me?"

Her eyes widened.

"I'm sorry. I guess that was a pretty direct question." He chuckled. "Well, let me start with how I feel about you. I care deeply for you and the girls. I like you very much. I think we make a good team. I'm very attracted to you. And I think we could...we would...eventually fall in love."

He hoped his blatant words wouldn't offend her, but they were honest and from his heart.

Nora smiled. "You know, that's funny, because I feel exactly the same way. But I've learned something about love. It's not a feeling, although there could be feelings with it. But I see it more as a decision. A commitment to meet the needs of someone else."

"Honestly, I don't know if I've ever been in love. I'm not even sure what it's supposed to look like. But I look at others—Silas and Kayla, Michael and Miriam, Paul and Jenny, my parents—and I want that. For us. So, I'm thinking. How do you feel about taking our relationship to the next level?"

"Which would be?"

"I really don't think dating would work for us." He smiled and caressed her cheek. "Our passions run too high."

"*Jah*, I've noticed that." Her smile was soft, bashful.

"I went and spoke with the bishop."

Her head shot up. "You did?"

"I did." He nodded. "I've been praying. And I'm seriously considering joining the church when fall rolls around."

"Are you, really?"

"I am. And after that, if you're agreeable, well—"

She nodded enthusiastically. "Yes, I would be agreeable to that."

"I might need someone to help me study the Dordrecht Confession, though."

"I might know someone who's willing." Her grin widened.

"Of course, I'd want you to talk to your girls about it to make sure they're cool with it. And I'll talk to Bailey." He rubbed his forehead. "And that's another thing. If we did, you know, would you be okay with Bailey moving in here—*if* she wanted to?"

"Of course. She's your daughter."

"She's also a teenager." He studied her.

"She'd be a great help."

"I have no doubt about that."

He blew out a breath. He hadn't even realized how nervous he was. "I should go."

He rose from the table. "But before I say goodbye, I'd like to claim one of those kisses."

She walked him to the door, then stepped near. "I'd be happy to oblige."

Just one, he told himself. He drew her into his arms, leaned down, then pressed his lips to hers. If he only got one kiss tonight, he was going to make it good. After all, he'd be leaving for New Jersey soon and he wanted to leave her with something to remember him by.

He slipped his fingers from one hand under her *kapp*, and cradled her face with the other. He lifted her chin slightly, slanting his head so he could kiss her more fully, more deeply. She responded with enthusiasm equal to his. When she whimpered, he finally forced himself away.

"Was that kiss okay? I had to give you at least one before I leave." His fingers traced her lips.

She was trembling. *Ach*, he'd overdone it. "That was *one*?" She whispered.

"I can't wait to make you my *fraa*." He pulled her into an embrace. "I'm going to miss you while I'm gone."

"I'll miss you too. Please hurry back."

TWENTY-FOUR

Bailey stared out the window down the driveway, bouncing on her toes.

"Calm down, Bailey. Your new *dat* will be here soon enough," Judah said.

Technically, he was her *old* dad, but she wouldn't get into that with her younger brother. "I know. I'm just anxious to go. I can't wait to see everybody in Pennsylvania and see where my dad works. It's gonna be so much fun."

"That's not fair. How did you get *two* dads?"

She sighed. "It's complicated, Judah. And you probably wouldn't understand it, so I'm not going to explain," she said in her big sister voice.

If she ever did leave here to live with Dad, she was going to miss her siblings. Make that stepsiblings.

Something flashed outside. "He's here!"

Bailey quickly hugged everyone. Why did she feel

like she was setting off on a new adventure, a new life? Maybe because she was.

Hopefully, this would allow her heart to heal and she wouldn't lament Timothy so much. She shook her head. She refused to dwell on him right now when the adventure of her life was about to begin. Who knew? Maybe she'd meet a new boy in Pennsylvania. One that didn't care that she'd ever been *Englisch*.

"You ready, Bay?"

She spun around. Dad was beaming. He must be as excited about this trip as she was.

"I sure am!"

Judah moaned and rolled his eyes. "It's *all* she's been talking about. And when she gets back I'm going to have to hear about it again for weeks."

"Don't be so dramatic, Judah. Besides, you love it when I tell you stories. And I'll have lots of stories to tell."

"We might even spend a day at the beach!" Dad said.

Mamm inhaled a sharp breath and Dad's gaze shot to her.

All of a sudden, it seemed like the room went quiet. Like a snowy winter day when not even the clip-clop of buggy horses could be heard. What was going on?

Dad's face darkened. "Uh, I'm sorry. I shouldn't

have—I didn't even think."

Silas stepped near and squeezed his shoulder. "It's all right. That's in the past now, remember?" He eyed *Mamm*.

Mamm recovered. "Yes, Bailey will love the beach. She hasn't been since she was little." She turned to Bailey and smiled. "You'll like the water on the east coast. It's a lot warmer than where we used to go in California."

"I hardly remember."

"You'll have a good time," *Mamm* assured.

"I know I will." She smiled at Dad. "Are we ready to go?"

Dad rubbed his hands together. "I'm ready whenever you are."

Mamm and Silas and all the *kinner* walked out to the car with them. Silas held little Aaron in his arms, and *Mamm* held Lucas by the hand.

Dad looked at Silas. "Would you pray for us before we go?"

Silas smiled and nodded. "I'd be happy to. I'll be praying for you while you're gone as well."

They all bowed their heads while Silas prayed aloud. Bailey said her own prayer, asking God to not only give them a safe and fun trip, but to keep her family here safe as well.

Mamm embraced her tightly. When she pulled back, tears shimmered in her eyes.

Bailey whispered in her ear, "You're not losing me, *Mamm*."

She brushed away a tear. "I know. I've just never been away from you for this long. I'll miss you."

"I'll miss you too, *Mamm*. Dad will take good care of me." She smiled.

Mamm glanced at Dad. "I know he will."

Ach, it was so good to see them getting along now. At one point, it seemed impossible. But *Gott* had been good. He'd given them healing.

Bailey waved through the window as she and Dad drove down the driveway. He stopped at the end of the lane to allow a horse and buggy to pass. She gasped when the driver looked her way, then scowled. *Ach, Timothy!*

"You know that boy?" Dad turned out onto the road, soon passing by Timothy's buggy.

Timothy stared the entire time.

"That's Timothy."

"Ah, the sort-of boyfriend."

"No. He's not my boyfriend at all. Anymore. He has someone else now."

"Oh." Dad frowned. "I'm sorry, Bay."

She pressed her lips together, resisting the urge to

glance into the rearview mirror before Dad turned onto the main road. "It's one of the reasons I was so eager to come with you. I hate seeing him with someone else. It feels like an elephant stepping on my heart."

"That sounds painful." He winced.

"It is."

"Hey, I know you probably don't want to hear this right now. But there are a lot of other boys out there, hoping to meet a nice girl like you."

Jah, but they weren't Timothy—the one she loved.

"Maybe God has someone better in mind for you. You can trust Him."

"You're right."

"Not to change the subject, but I need to talk to you about something."

"I don't mind a different subject."

"I wanted to let you know that I'm planning to become Plain again."

A smile spread across her face. "Really?"

"Yes, in the Eichers' district."

"I'm so happy to hear that!"

"And I'm thinking of settling down." He glanced at her. "How do you feel about Elnora Schwartz?"

"Nora? I like her. She's nice."

"I like her too."

"You're going to marry her, aren't you?"

"I hope so."

"I knew it! I told *Mamm* and Silas that you were going to become Amish and marry Nora."

He chuckled. "You did? How did you know?"

"I'm a good guesser."

"I was also thinking...I talked with Nora about this already...that if you wanted to come and live with us, we wouldn't be against it. Of course, you'd have to ask your folks. I know your mother is awfully attached to you."

"*Jah*, she is. But I eventually have to find my own way."

"Maybe we should pray about it."

"I like that idea."

⁂

Their two weeks in New Jersey and Pennsylvania had flown by, just like most of his life, Josiah realized. He glanced across the car at his daughter, who was now asleep. How had this girl grown up so quickly? Where had the years gone?

He knew that he'd missed out on most of her life. It was something he'd always regret. But they had here and now. And by the grace of God, he would make the most of it.

Truthfully, he was excited to see what God had planned up ahead. He'd likely be married by the end of this year. He'd be a member of the *g'may*. He'd be joining his friends Michael, Silas, Paul, and Sammy for weekly Bible studies and growing in his knowledge of God.

And then there was Bailey. She'd likely be finding a life mate and beginning a new chapter of her life. Chances are, they'd have *kinner* the same age. Imagine that! And if his friends' happiness was any indication of what he had to look forward to, well, he was ready to dive right in.

And that was exactly what he planned to do.

EPILOGUE

The following spring...

Josiah reached for his *fraa's* hand, intertwining his fingers with hers, as they gently swayed on Sammy Eicher's porch swing. He glanced toward the yard, where Bailey pushed his stepdaughters on the swings. His heart couldn't get any fuller. Especially since this morning, when Nora whispered in his ear that he was going to be a daddy again—but it was like the first time, since he hadn't gotten a chance at raising Bailey.

Michael stepped onto the porch at the same time Nora stood.

Nora squeezed his hand. "I'm going to see if Miriam needs help with anything."

Michael smiled. "I'm sure she'll appreciate that. She was up half the night with the *boppli*." Their little one had arrived about three weeks ago.

Josiah couldn't wait to hold his own *boppli* in his arms. He was tempted to tell his friend about their surprise, but he kept it to himself.

"What's got you so quiet?" Michael sank down next to him.

He hoped the swing would hold the both of them.

"Just thinking about things. About life. About God's goodness."

"He sure is good, isn't He?"

Josiah set the swing in motion with the toe of his boot. "I felt like I had been in a boat on the sea most of my life, never really going anywhere, just drifting. But now? Now, I feel like I've finally arrived at a destination. And it feels good. I'm no longer a drifter. For the first time in my life, I feel like I'm home."

Michael smiled back at him. "I know exactly what you mean."

THE END

Thanks for reading!
Word of mouth is one of the best forms of
advertisement and a HUGE blessing to the
author. If you enjoyed this book, **please** consider
leaving a review, sharing on social media, and
telling your reading friends.

THANK YOU!

DISCUSSION QUESTIONS

1. We first read about Josiah Beachy in *The Trespasser*, Amish Country Brides, book one. What were your initial thoughts of him at the end of that book, provided you've read it?

2. Bailey is heartbroken when Timothy shares his news with her. Do you think his parents were just in attempting to protect their son?

3. When Bailey discovers her mother's secret, she's unsure how to handle it. Have you ever discovered someone else's secret? How did you handle it?

4. Since leaving his community, Josiah has been (mostly) estranged from his friends. Have you been estranged from friends who were once close?

5. When Elnora and Josiah first meet, she accepts a ride with him. Have you ever accepted a ride with

a stranger? Did you live to tell about it? (Just kidding.) Real question: Would you do it again?

6. Josiah and Nora seemed to click instantly. Have you ever begun a relationship that way?

7. Bailey was eager to share Jesus' love with her father. If you are a Christian, have you ever shared Jesus with someone? Did that person accept Christ?

8. Josiah had decided he wasn't interested in religion since he'd grown up in it. But Silas showed him that salvation was not a result of being religious, it was about God's gift to mankind. Have you personally accepted God's gift? If you'd like to, please see Chapter Twenty.

9. What were your final thoughts of Josiah Beachy?

10. Who was your favorite character in *The Drifter*? Why?

A SPECIAL THANK YOU

I'd like to take this time to thank everyone that had any involvement in this book and its production, including my Mom and Dad, who have always been supportive of my writing, my longsuffering Family— especially my handsome, encouraging Hubby, my Amish and former-Amish friends who have helped immensely in my understanding of the Amish ways, my supportive Pastor and Church family, my Proofreaders, my Editor, my CIA Facebook author friends who have been a tremendous help, my wonderful Readers who buy, read, offer great input, and leave encouraging reviews and emails, my awesome Launch Team who, I'm confident, will 'Sprede the Word' about *The Drifter*! And last, but certainly not least, I'd like to thank my *Precious LORD and SAVIOUR JESUS CHRIST*, for without Him, none of this would have been possible!

If you haven't joined my Facebook reader group, you may do so here:
https://www.facebook.com/groups/379193966104149/

GET THE NEXT BOOK...

The Giver (Amish Country Brides)

Returning home for the holidays is bittersweet for Bailey Miller. While she loves her mother and stepfather's family and wants to spend time with them, she knows she'll inevitably run into Timothy Stoltzfoos—the man who betrayed her and broke her heart. Although Timothy's available now, she's not interested. At least, that's what she tells herself. She's promised to Mark Petersheim—a man she doesn't love nearly as much as she'd once loved Timothy. But he's a nice man and will make a good husband.

Timothy Stoltzfoos messed up big time when he chose MaryAnn Kinsinger over Bailey Miller. It had been four years since he'd heard she'd left for the *Englisch* world to live with her father in New Jersey. But now she's back and she's Amish again—and engaged to be married to an Amish man in a nearby district. He knows Bailey would never give him a second chance, but Christmas was a time for miracles, wasn't it?

NOW available for preorder!

An Unexpected Christmas Gift

Janie Mishler is content with her life as an *alt maedel* helping out at her father's Amish dry goods store, but she's always wondered "what if?" What if Elson hadn't passed on? What if she'd met someone else? What if she could raise a family of her own? But with each year that passes, Janie relinquishes her unfulfilled dreams. That is, until she receives an unexpected Christmas gift from someone who appears to be a stranger.

Rob Zehr put his Amish life behind him to forget about his painful past and follow his lifelong dream of becoming a pilot. Although he still communicates with his family, he has no desire to return to his old lifestyle. When he receives a mysterious note in the mail, he responds out of sheer intrigue. He never imagined that the note's writer could be the one to draw him back to his roots and open his heart to the possibility of love again.

Are their circumstances merely coincidence? Or could it be God's unseen hand working a Christmas miracle?

Featured in the
Amish Christmas Miracles Collection

Spend Christmas in Amish country.

As snow falls softly outside the window, curl up by the fire with this collection of *14 stories by your favorite Amish fiction authors.*

Let them transport you to Amish communities all across the country.

Travel to small towns where horses clip-clop down the road, farms dot the snow-covered landscape, and families gather to celebrate the real meaning of **Christmas.**

Sigh over sweet stories that touch your heart. Laugh, cry, rejoice, and smile as couples renew their faith and find their perfect soul mates.

These heartwarming tales of faith, hope, love, and Christmas miracles are our special gift to you.

Release Date: November 10, 2020
NOW available for preorder!

Made in the USA
Las Vegas, NV
05 November 2020

10599385R00141